Half-Pint Fisherman

Books by Elizabeth Rider Montgomery

KEYS TO NATURE'S SECRETS

THE STORY BEHIND GREAT INVENTIONS

THE STORY BEHIND GREAT STORIES

THE STORY BEHIND GREAT MEDICAL DISCOVERIES

THE STORY BEHIND GREAT BOOKS

THE STORY BEHIND MODERN BOOKS

THE STORY BEHIND MUSICAL INSTRUMENTS

THREE MILES AN HOUR

HALF-PINT FISHERMAN

Half-Pint Fisherman

ELIZABETH RIDER MONTGOMERY

Illustrated by Gerald McCann

DODD, MEAD & COMPANY, NEW YORK, 1956

*To my friends and neighbors
at Alki, especially the boys and girls*

CONTENTS

ILLUSTRATIONS

Half-Pint Fisherman

1.   CHEERS FOR HARBOR HIGH

"THE NEXT CONTESTANT," ANNOUNCED the freshman class president, "is Barton Skinner."

An expectant titter ran through the group of boys who had gathered, this first week of school, to watch the preliminary tryouts for cheer leaders. Everybody at Harbor High School knew that Barton Skinner was good for a laugh anytime—and that was all the little shrimp *was* good for, in their eyes.

Bart slid out of his seat and walked briskly to the front of the room, outwardly calm and confident, inwardly tense and excited. This was his big chance, this cheer leader job. This was something spectacular which he could do fully as well as fellows a foot higher than he.

The little fellow grinned, and met answering smiles from the other boys. Vic Anderson, the class president, who was Bart's chum, gave him an especially warm grin. Only Mr. Boone, the principal of Harbor High (acting as faculty advisor for the group), gazed back at Bart soberly.

1

Bart's grin widened. He knew why old Boone-goon looked so sour: the principal was thinking of the first day of school, when Bart had sketched dozens of fish on the big map of Washington State which hung in the hall. Bart hadn't meant to ruin the old map; he had done it just for a laugh. Too bad old Boone had to be the faculty sponsor for yell leader.

"Go to it, Half-Pint!" called a raucous voice from the back row.

Bart's grin did not waver, but he writhed inwardly. He ought to be used to that repulsive nickname by now; he had heard it often enough. Yet it never failed to irritate him, to remind him of what he spent his days trying to forget: that he hadn't grown a single inch in two years.

"Let's try 'Razzle-Dazzle.'" Bart's voice sounded higher than ever in his own ears, almost squeaky. "Let's really put it over, fellows. Come on, now."

The boys rose obediently but warily, waiting for the inevitable joker.

The would-be cheer leader swung his arms in big circles. He rose on his toes and began the yell.

"Give 'em the ax, the ax, the ax. . . ." Bart's hands chopped the air in front of him in perfect rhythm, his feet keeping step in a sharp backward kick—but he yelled entirely alone. His high voice echoed thinly in the big room. His reputation as a clown made the others cautious of joining something that might turn the laugh on them.

Bart stopped. Hands on his slim hips, he looked around the group.

"This isn't supposed to be a solo, you know. How about

2

a little cooperation?"

Again he started the yell. This time Vic, the class president, joined him. Good old Vic! Bart could always count on him. One by one the others opened their mouths. The volume of sound doubled and redoubled. Now they were in the swing!

Gradually Bart increased the tempo. The boys took fire from his enthusiasm and followed him to a man. The cheer finished on a tremendous shout, with Bart leaping in the air and clicking his heels twice before landing lightly on his toes.

Everybody clapped, except Mr. Boone. Bart bowed and smiled and wiped the perspiration from his brow.

"Let's try the 'Cannon' now."

It was a difficult yell, but Bart led it expertly. He finished with a perfect cartwheel and took his seat amid a storm of applause. Even Mr. Boone clapped for him.

Bart mopped his brow again and congratulated himself silently. He had shown them, all right. They wouldn't dare pass him by now. He was certain to be chosen cheer leader. Then perhaps those guys who called him, so condescendingly, "Half-Pint," would realize that size isn't everything.

"The next contestant," Vic announced, "is Stephen Huber."

Scornfully Bart watched big hulking Steve, a newcomer to Harbor City, stumble over his own feet as he clambered out of his seat and lumbered down the aisle. That dumb cluck a cheer leader? Why, he had two left hands, and feet like rowboats, so big he couldn't get them off the ground. All he had in his favor was a voice loud enough for a foghorn. Bart had nothing to fear from Steve, he thought complacently.

How huge and clumsy the fellow looked! All arms and legs, and obviously wondering what to do with them. Bart laughed aloud, and Steve grinned sheepishly.

Then Steve announced his yell—and suddenly his awkwardness disappeared. His oversize arms and legs and his booming voice worked together amazingly. Who would have suspected the big fellow had such a good sense of rhythm?

When the cheer ended, Steve's gawkiness returned. He grinned sheepishly at the applause. Couldn't he even take a bow gracefully?

All the fellows gave Steve a big hand as he ambled back to his seat after leading a second cheer. Mr. Boone clapped as hard as anyone. Bart joined in the applause; he couldn't let them think he envied Steve, for of course he didn't. Envy that big lunk? What a stupid idea!

Vic, the chairman, looked at his list. "The next contestant . . ."

Bart slumped down in his seat, not listening. His mind raced back over the last two years, to the time when he was as big as the other boys. In those days he had been a part of every school activity, every neighborhood project. He had been the recognized leader of his class and of the South Cove gang. He had organized the vacant lot ball team and the Saturday Bike Club. He had felt competent and adequate in those days. That was long before Steve had moved into the neighborhood.

Then, one by one, the other boys had begun to grow by

4

leaps and bounds. New pants, in a few months' time, would hit them at the ankles. They outgrew their shoes and jackets and shirts long before they wore them out.

Bart glared at the red zipper jacket on the desk in front of him. His mother had bought it two years ago, but it still fitted him perfectly. No matter how fast the other kids grew, *he* stayed the same. No matter how deep their voices became, *his* remained high and reedy, like a child's. Yet he was practically the same age as the rest of the gang; he would be fourteen in two more months.

Oh, it wasn't fair! Why couldn't he grow like other kids?

The try-outs ended at last. With a wave to Vic, Bart hurried out. He was already half an hour late for his job at the Malt Shop, the corner soda fountain.

The little shop bulged with loud-voiced students; it was Harbor High's favorite after-school hangout. Mr. Willoughby greeted Bart with a sigh of relief.

"Well, at last! Four chocolate malts and three cokes—and hurry! They're way ahead of me." The bald-headed manager reached for a soda glass and the ice cream scoop. "And no time for clowning, mind you!"

Bart slipped on his white apron, washed his hands quickly, and dashed behind the fountain. Before Mr. Willoughby had finished fixing the soda, he had the malts spinning and had begun on the cokes.

The juke box blared a Hit Parade tune. Mr. Willoughby's voice rose above the din of chatter and rival music. "What made you so late, Bart?"

Bart's hands did not falter in their deft manipulation of

glasses and faucets. "I told you I'd be late today, Mr. Willoughby."

"Well, don't let it happen again," his employer grumbled.

Bart started to say it would soon be a regular occurrence, when he became cheer leader, but he held his tongue. Mr. Willoughby might get someone else for this job, and Bart wanted to hold onto it as long as possible. He liked it.

The press of orders had eased up a bit now. Bart began to play up to his audience. He drew each coke with a zip and a split-second timing that stopped just short of running the glass over, and served it with a flourish. He tossed each coin high in the air before ringing up the sale.

Another group came through the open door. Steve and Lexy Jensen, followed by Vic. Bart frowned. How come Lexy was with Steve? Bart considered his blonde neighbor Lexy his own special girl, although he seldom dated anyone. Living next door to each other since they were kids . . .

"Hi, Bart." Lexy's warm smile transformed her round face. "I'll have a coke."

"Make it two." Steve, close behind her, plunked down coins for both drinks with so much force everything on the counter jumped. Bart resisted an impulse to glare at the presumptuous big fellow, and served the cokes with great ceremony. Steve followed Lexy over to the juke box corner. Bart didn't hear Vic's request for a milk-shake.

"Come out of the clouds, Bart," Vic's quiet voice admonished. "I want a vanilla shake."

"Oh! Sure." Bart brought his mind back to his business. He raised his voice deliberately. "I'll make you a super-

Steve followed Lexy over to the juke box corner. Bart didn't hear Vic's request for a milk-shake.

duper shake, Vic. Watch this."

Fully half the room heeded his admonition to watch him. Stimulated, as always, by an audience, Bart really put on an act. His hands moved with lightning-quick precision to get the mixer can and open the ice cream bin. Wielding the scoop with his right hand, he held the container far to the left.

"Watch it, Bart!" warned Mr. Willoughby, but Bart did not heed. He tossed the ball of frozen cream into the air. Its arc was wider than he anticipated. Frantically he tried to get the container under it as it fell, but the ice cream missed by an inch. It landed on the floor.

Mr. Willoughby snatched the container out of Bart's hand. "That's the second time this week! I'll make this shake while you clean up the mess." His voice crackled with indignation. "And the next time you let ice cream land on the floor, Barton Skinner, you'll land on the sidewalk yourself —outside!"

Bart ducked down to take care of the messy floor, glad of an excuse to hide his flaming face. By the time he finished, he had recovered his self-possession. He whistled a tango in unison with the juke box.

There was a lull in business at the fountain. For the first time Bart noticed a new poster on the side wall.

"Kids' Fishing Derby, October 12. All boys and girls between the ages of ten and fifteen eligible. First prize, light-weight racing bike. Other prizes include . . ."

Bart read no farther. Brother! This was a chance to shine which he had forgotten about: the Kids' Fishing Derby!

8

Fishing was one sport where size did not matter; know-how was the only thing that counted. He had as good a chance as anybody to win the Derby.

His thoughts on the fishing derby, Bart forgot to show off his dexterity as he served the next few customers.

The whole town turned out for that Kids' Fishing Derby It was the big event of the fall in the little Puget Sound city. Business men put up the prizes, a dozen or more; the boat house supplied boats; the Harbor Patrol supervised the fishing area; the police department shot off the start and finish signals, and stood by for any emergency. The women of the community served refreshments to the young fishermen and their parents and well-wishers. And every kid who could handle a rod and reel fished for all he was worth on that day, whether or not he ever baited a hook the rest of the year.

As for the top winners! Bart's eyes glistened as he remembered what a big play the first prize winners got in the newspapers and on the radio. They were always interviewed in front of the crowd as their prizes were awarded. The papers always carried big photographs of them with their winning fish and their prizes. This year they would probably be interviewed on television, too.

Bart could see himself now, facing the television cameras, at ease, laughing, telling how he had caught the tremendous salmon he held up for the entire community to see.

The juke box fell silent. An argument across the room caught Bart's attention.

"He hasn't got a chance!"

9

"He has, too! What'll you bet he wins?"

"Aw, Steve's the one."

"Sure. It's between Steve and Bart."

Busy at the fountain, Bart strained his ears to hear. Those fellows were talking about the contest for cheer leader, of course. So they thought Steve had a chance against him, did they? What a laugh!

"Gosh, I hope he doesn't get it. He's already so stuck on himself."

"He'll be worse if he loses."

"Yeah. A poor sport."

A mocking voice chanted, "Barton Skinner's a lousy winner."

Another voice took it up. "He's not a snoozer, but a darn poor loser."

A burst of raucous laughter greeted this sally.

Bart almost dropped a glass. Why, the nerve of those guys! He took so long drawing a coke that his customer reminded him impatiently.

Fuming, Bart began to clean the fountain. So the fellows thought Steve was a good sport, huh? Well, he'd show them how wrong they were. He'd beat Steve as cheer leader if it was the last thing he did! And he'd nose him out with Lexy, too, by jiminy!

Then the kids would see what kind of a loser Steve was. They'd find out who was a poor sport!

2. BART STICKS HIS NECK OUT

AS HE ALWAYS DID WHEN HE DRESSED FOR school in the morning, Bart looked anxiously in his mirror, hoping to see some signs that he had begun to grow. But every morning he saw the same thing: baby-smooth face, thick dark hair, carefully brushed in the latest style, alert brown eyes. That much wasn't so bad. It was the short, slight figure, in its bright sport shirt sprinkled with eye-catching campaign buttons, and size ten slacks showing just a glimpse of brilliant socks, that bothered him. Not a bit taller than he was yesterday—and the day before—and the day before that.

Bart shook his fist at his own image, neat and clean and handsome though it was. He scowled. It wasn't fair. He followed all the health rules: good food, plenty of sleep and exercise, and all of that routine, yet he didn't grow. And Steve, who was only two months older than he, and who ate tons of candy bars and cokes and stuff that wasn't good for you—Steve grew like Jack's beanstalk.

11

As he passed his younger brother's room, Bart caught sight of Eddie, staring anxiously in his own mirror. The expression on his face duplicated the one that had looked back at Bart. Could Eddie, too, be worried about not growing big?

But Eddie was barely twelve. He had plenty of time to grow.

Bart went into the kitchen. Little Mrs. Skinner was scurrying back and forth busily from sink to range.

"Good morning, Son. Hungry?" This was her usual question.

"Yes." Bart flung his books on a chair. "Breakfast ready?"

"Almost."

Quiet footsteps announced Eddie's entrance. He came into the kitchen, shoelaces dragging, hair in his eyes, and threw down the empty canvas bag in which he would carry his papers after school.

Bart surveyed him disapprovingly. "Why don't you ever comb your hair and tie your shoelaces?" he asked, smugly conscious of his own neat appearance and carefully combed hair.

Eddie did not answer. He never answered when you talked to him.

"Set the table, boys," said Mrs. Skinner. "Breakfast's ready."

"It's Eddie's turn," Bart said quickly. "I did it yesterday."

"Then you'll wipe the dishes tonight," his mother agreed.

Eddie smiled secretively, and Bart turned away. Why hadn't he kept his mouth shut? Dishes!

Dr. Skinner came into the kitchen. "Good morning,

12

everybody."

The sight of his handsome, strapping father never failed to rouse in Bart a surge of pride and a sharp pang of envy. He would give anything to be like his father, to have people tip their heads back to look up at him, to have them defer to his opinions.

Suddenly Bart noticed that he and his mother and his brother were all three practically the same height, a foot shorter than Dr. Skinner. How big and important his father must feel, to be the only *man* in a family of runts! Some people had all the luck!

All the neighborhood children took the same bus in the mornings. As they waited at the corner, laughing and shouting, pushing and shoving, Bart noticed for the first time that the seventh and eighth graders, as well as the high school boys, were growing out of their pants legs and their jacket sleeves. Only Eddie—and he, himself—remained pint-sized in a neighborhood of quarts and gallons. In a rare burst of fellow feeling, Bart smiled at his young brother. The surprise and gratitude in the smile he received in return pricked Bart's conscience. He ought to pay more attention to the kid; Eddie wasn't having it so good these days, either.

The bus drew up to the corner and stopped. There was a new driver.

One of the younger boys had the seat next to the window that Bart wanted, so he sat on the youngster and jumped up and down until the boy got up and left the seat to him. Bart looked out the window. A flash of red caught his eye. Lexy was running for the bus. On the seat beside him, Bart placed the box of fishing tackle which he was taking to school to use with his hobby talk. He would save that seat for Lexy.

The driver moved his hand to put the bus in gear. Quickly Bart reached up and jerked the stop cord.

"Who did that?" growled the bus driver.

"There's a girl running for the bus," Bart called.

"Well, why couldn't you say so?"

Lexy climbed up the steps, flushed and breathless. To get her attention, Bart put two fingers in his mouth and whistled shrilly.

"Stop that racket," snapped the bus driver over his shoulder, making no move to start the bus. "I'm not going to drive with that whistle splitting my eardrums."

Bart whistled again.

"Pipe down, Runt," growled one of the older boys. "We want to get to school."

The other boys took it up. "Cut it out, Bart." "Act your age, Half-Pint." "Grow up, Shrimp."

Bart made faces at all of them. He wiggled his ears and contorted his mouth until all the children were laughing.

Lexy came down the aisle. Bart stopped his clowning and removed his fishing gear from the seat beside him, but Lexy passed him by, nose in the air, as if she had not seen him. She sat down in the seat Steve vacated for her.

All the way to school Bart fumed silently. So Lexy thought she could ignore him, did she? And Steve thought he was top guy? Well, let them wait. They would see who was top guy in this neighborhood. He would show them!

14

English class lacked only ten minutes of being over when the teacher called on Bart for his hobby talk. But he liked it that way. Now that the class had sat through Lexy's clear but commonplace discussion of miniature-collecting, and Al's slow-moving talk on model-building, and Parker's halting and boring account of record-collecting, they would really appreciate a live-wire talk on a real sport.

Carrying his fishing gear, Bart walked briskly to the front of the room. Anticipatory grins flashed from face to face.

"Fishing is a universal sport and a grand hobby," he began, with a little preliminary ear-wiggling that set them all to laughing. "It has many advantages. First, it takes you into the open air, which is good for you. Second, it doesn't cost anything, once you get your gear—and you can start with inexpensive stuff. And third . . ." Bart paused. What was the third reason he had planned to give? Certainly he had never intended to reveal his own main reason for liking to fish: that a little guy could be just as good a fisherman as a big fellow. What other reason had he planned to mention?

Oh, yes, now he remembered. "Third, you get something useful out of it, something your whole family can enjoy. That is, if you're lucky."

The class smiled. A few chuckled. Bart went on.

"Here in the Northwest we have opportunities for several different kinds of fishing. You can follow the streams on foot for fly-fishing, you can do still-fishing on the lakes, or you can stick to salmon fishing in salt water. Salmon fishing is my favorite hobby and that's what I shall talk about."

15

He put his rod together and attached the reel. "In salmon fishing, you use a rod like this and a reel with a drag, or a brake, on it. That's so your line won't pay out too fast. Be sure the reel is fastened tight. It's no fun to lose it when you are playing a big salmon."

He opened his tackle box and took out leader, sinker and dodger. Talking as he worked, he attached the objects to his line, explaining each item.

"This piece of lead is called a sinker. It weights your line down so the bait will go down in the water where the salmon will see it. This metal gadget" . . . he held up a shiny six-inch oblong with a hole in each end . . . "is called a dodger or flasher. It has to be kept bright and shining so that it will catch the light and attract the salmon."

Bart had finished rigging his line now. He held it in his hand as he went on talking. "In salmon fishing, you can troll or spin or mooch." Titters from the class. Bart took it up quickly. "I said 'mooch' not 'smooch.' " Loud laughter from the class. He really had his audience now; they would listen to every word, hoping for another joke.

"In trolling, you use a motor or else row. Your boat must move slowly through the water. That makes your bait move, of course. I like herring for bait, on a double hook like this. Sorry I couldn't bring herring to show you, but I was afraid the teachers might not appreciate fish smell all over the place." More titters.

"Baiting is simple." He pantomimed the process. "When your hooks are baited right, one below the other, and your dodger is set properly, and you have the right amount of leader and the proper sinker, your herring moves back and

16

forth through the water and looks like a live herring swimming. The salmon strikes at it, the hooks catch in his throat, and you have him."

Suddenly Bart became conscious that Steve was watching him intently. What could that big clumsy fellow be up to? Well, he couldn't stop to worry about it now. He had to get on with his talk.

"That's where your fun starts. There's nothing like the thrill of playing a big salmon—nothing I know of, anyway. You can't bring him in right away. If you try, he will snap your line and maybe your rod. You have to tire him out, so you give him all the line he wants. Give him enough rope and he'll hang himself." He grinned and his audience grinned back.

"After your fish has dived and swum for a few minutes— or an hour, depending on his size—he gets tired. Then you can reel him in. But you have to watch. Maybe he is just trying to catch you off guard. The trick is to be smarter than the fish. When you are sure he is really tired, then you reel in until he is close to the boat. You get your net under him, or gaff him, and there you are!"

Bart paused to look at his notes. He wasn't quite up to form this morning. Not nearly as clever and funny as he had planned to be. But at least the class was listening.

"Some people don't use bait in trolling. They use either a metal lure or a plug." Bart took from his tackle box a small piece of metal, in the shape of a fish, with a hook on the end of it. "This is a spoon, which flips back and forth and attracts the salmon. Sometimes a spoon will work when they won't strike on herring, but I think it is usually the other way around.

"In spinning, you don't use a flasher. Just leader and herring. And you don't use a motor or oars; you anchor or drift with the tide. You cast out and let your bait settle to the bottom, then you bring it in a little at a time. This action of the bait shooting toward the surface, a few feet at a time, attracts the salmon."

A few pointers on mooching and he was through. But what was that joke he had intended finishing with? For the life of him, Bart couldn't remember. "Well," he ended lamely. "I guess that's all. Any questions?"

Steve spoke up instantly. "Why don't you use bait with a spoon?"

"You don't need it. A spoon is made to *look* like bait."

"What do you do when a fish bites?" Steve again.

"Well, you don't bite him back," Bart retorted. Loud laughter. "I told you what to do; let him have as much line as he wants."

"But—*how* do you let him?"

Bart glared at Steve. Was the guy deliberately heckling him? "Look," he said sharply, "when you hook a fish he tries to get away. He swims, as fast as he can, away from the boat. Since he has swallowed the hooks, he takes them with him. And since the hooks are fastened to the line," holding up the hooks, "he pulls on the line as he swims away. That makes the line unwind from your reel, like this." With exaggerated patience Bart pulled several yards of line from his reel to demonstrate.

The entire class was giggling now at the elaborately detailed explanation. Only Steve sat, serious and frowning,

18

taking in every word, every gesture.

"But how can you tell when the fish has had enough line?" Steve persisted when Bart paused. "What if you give him . . ."

His patience gone, Bart interrupted sardonically, "There isn't time in this class to teach you how to fish, Steve. If you don't know how, come out on the bay with me Saturday morning, and I'll *show* you."

Steve's face lighted up. "You will?"

Bart bit his lip. The dummy had taken him up on an offer that was supposed merely to hold Steve up for ridicule. Bart smiled wryly. He would have to go through with it now.

"Sure. Meet you on our beach at 5:30 A. M.—if you can get up before breakfast."

The bell rang before anyone could ask another question. Bart gathered up his fishing gear and started for his next class, not at all pleased with the turn events had taken. Rats! Because he had goofed off, he had to take Steve out fishing. He would have that dumb cluck on his hands for a couple of hours. Why had he stuck his neck out?

3.   BEACH PARTY BUSINESS
AND MONKEY BUSINESS

BART HURRIED STRAIGHT HOME FROM
school, for Lexy was having a beach party, taking advantage of an unexpected half holiday—school had closed at noon today because of a county-wide teachers' meeting.

Bart was certainly glad Mr. Willoughby had decided to close up the Malt Shop as he did on Saturdays and regular school holidays, for otherwise he would have missed the best part of the party.

He went directly to Lexy's house, two doors up the beach from his own home. Lexy, in shorts and tee-shirt, opened the door, a welcoming smile on her round face.

"Need any help getting ready for the party?" Bart asked. "Wood for the fire or stuff?"

"Sure. Let's go down on the beach and fix things up."

The beach in front of Lexy's house provided the best spot for wiener roasts in the entire cove—a deep half-sandy arc of beach that the high tides did not touch except during midwinter storms. There was a great driftwood snag that had been used as a backlog for more beach fires than anyone could count; a mammoth log, half buried in sand, against the bulkhead, which made a fair serving table; and driftwood of all shapes and sizes for firewood.

Bart and Lexy cleared a space around the blackened snag for the fire which they would build later. They pulled and tugged and rolled logs into place for seats. They found a big flat-topped chunk for an extra table. Then they gathered wood for the fire. Lexy picked up small stuff for kindling, and Bart concentrated on bark, which held the heat and made excellent coals for roasting wieners and marshmallows.

As he worked, Bart felt warm and good all through. It was not only the physical exertion, but the feeling of companionship with this girl he had grown up with. From the time they were toddlers, building castles in the sand on this very beach, wading in the summer swells, he and Lexy had been pals. They had always worked and played together like two boys—until Steve had moved into the neighborhood. Bart frowned as he unearthed a particularly big hunk of thick cedar bark and threw it up on the beach to dry. He wished Steve would go back where he came from. How come he had moved here to Harbor City? Bart realized he knew very little about his rival. He only knew that he did not like him, and that he intended to win out over him in the cheer leader contest.

Lexy brushed the sand from her hands and surveyed the results of their efforts, just as the first guests arrived. "There," she said with obvious satisfaction. "That's a good job. Thanks a lot, Bart."

"Okay. Back in a few minutes, Lexy." Bart went on home, happily confident that this last beach party of the season would be the best one yet.

The beach party was in full swing. The swimmers had raced each other out to the various sailboats and cruisers which beach residents kept anchored offshore in the summer. They had dived off the boats. They had paddled around the cove on driftwood logs, pushing each other off, tumbling and splashing. They had dived for bright pebbles and gleaming white shells on the bottom. Now the young people sat in the sun on the Jensens' wooden seawall, swinging their legs, laughing and shouting, or they lay on towels in the yard, lazy and quiet, while their bathing suits dried.

All except Bart. He stayed on the beach, skipping stones across the water, turning cartwheels on the sand, urging the others to join him in another race, taunting them with laziness.

Bart had been having a wonderful time all afternoon. He had returned to the beach party in a ridiculous get-up that set everybody to laughing: a striped bathrobe over his bathing trunks, his dad's discarded straw hat on his head, and a swagger cane from last year's County Fair in his hand.

Yes, his performance had been a riot. He had pretended he was going to dive off the bulkhead, still with bathrobe and hat on. He had used his cane to trip the girls as they ran out in the water. And he had given the gang an upside-down demonstration of yell-leading, standing on his head

22

Bart had been having a wonderful time all afternoon. He had returned to the beach party in a ridiculous get-up that set everybody to laughing . . .

in the sand, with the bathrobe falling around him, keeping time with his waving feet.

Even after he stopped clowning and discarded the incongruous robe and hat, Bart continued to enjoy himself. A good swimmer from kindergarten days, he gave the bigger boys real competition in the swimming races, although he could never quite win; most of this group, having lived on or near the water all their lives, were completely at home in that element. No one objected seriously when Bart splashed water in a swimmer's face, or swam underneath a girl and pulled her feet down. It was all just good fun for young people who had been in and out of the water since they could remember.

Latecomers, carrying bathing suits and towels, continued to drift in. They went in the house to change to swimming things.

Then Steve arrived, dressed in good school slacks instead of blue jeans like the others. It seemed to Bart that the shout which greeted him was louder and warmer than anyone else had received. Certainly Lexy's face showed more pleasure than the laws of hospitality demanded. The sun, low now in the western sky across the bay, might as well have set, as far as Bart was concerned; the brightness and warmth of the day were over.

Steve greeted everybody with his slow, almost sheepish smile. He shook his head at suggestions of swimming. "I didn't bring my trunks."

Suddenly Bart decided he would get Steve in the water or know the reason why. He had never seen Steve swim. If he was as dumb in the water as he was about fishing . . .

24

Polly the giddy red-head who chummed with Lexy . . .

"I'll lend you a pair of mine."

Steve guffawed, and Bart flushed. He had stuck his neck out that time, all right. Steve couldn't begin to get into his trunks, of course.

Polly, the giddy red-head who chummed with Lexy, giggled shrilly. "Imagine Steve wearing Bart's clothes! I never heard of anything so funny in all my life!" The gang roared.

"I mean, you can wear a pair of my dad's," Bart explained, trying to smile as if he, too, thought the whole thing very funny.

Steve attempted to demur. It was too late to swim. He'd rather stay with the others. Bart's father might want to use his own swimming trunks.

The more Steve objected, the more determined Bart became to get him in the water. He scrambled over the bulkhead, caught Steve's arm, and led him across the intervening lawn to his own home, still protesting, but not pulling back.

"Like a puppy teasing a Great Dane," Bart heard silly Polly say with a giggle.

When Bart and Steve returned to the cove, three other latecomers were swimming toward an anchored boat. Steve looked gawkier and more ill at ease than ever in Dr. Skinner's green trunks. Bart splashed in knee-deep, and made a shallow dive into the bay. He swam swiftly out into deep water, then stopped to tread water. He called back to Steve.

"Come on, Steve. Dive in."

But Steve stood hesitantly at the water's edge, dabbling

26

one great toe tentatively in the gentle salt-water swells.

"It's cold," he protested.

Bart snorted. What did he expect Puget Sound water to be? Bath temperature? "It won't seem cold after you get wet. Dive in. Get wet all at once."

Steve took one reluctant step into the water . . . then another. The other boys joined their urging to Bart's, and Steve waded out until the water reached his waist . . . then his armpits. There he balked and stood, shivering. Although voices from both shore and bay prodded him, Steve made no move to venture any further.

Suddenly Bart drew a deep breath and dived. He swam under water toward shore. Silently he glided past Steve's legs and got behind him. Then he caught the big fellow by the ankles and jerked his feet out from under him. With a splash Steve went down. A shout of laughter went up from the watching crowd. Bart came to the surface and shook his dripping hair out of his eyes. Now maybe Steve would swim.

But something was wrong. Steve was not swimming! He threshed wildly around, gasping and choking. Why, he could not swim! He didn't even know how to get on his feet! And he was moving into deeper water with every wild splash.

Bart dived again and came up under Steve's head. Evading the threshing arms, he flung his own arm around the big boy's throat and clutched him tight. In an instant he had rolled Steve over on his back and was towing him to shore.

As Bart pulled him out of the water, the entire group crowded around. Steve had swallowed quite a bit of water and was sick and miserable, as well as shaking from fright. Lexy ran over to get Dr. Skinner.

For once, Bart had no longing for the spotlight. While his father checked the patient, and the others huddled close, sober and anxious, Bart slumped down alone on the wooden bulkhead. What a fool he was! If Steve had drowned, it would have been his fault. But how was he expected to know that Steve could not swim?

His conscience repeated the warning his father had often given him: "Never duck anyone unless you *know* he can swim." Well, he had learned his lesson the hard way.

He had better go home. He could not face the gang after this. Bart got to his feet slowly.

"There." Dr. Skinner's cheerful voice rose above the sudden babble on the beach. "You'll be all right, young man. Nothing wrong with you except you tried to swallow the entire bay."

Steve was on his feet now. Bart quickened his steps toward home.

"Hey, Bart!" It was Steve's deep voice, a bit shaky but loud as ever. Bart stopped. Now he was in for it. The big guy was going to tell him off. Bart squared his shoulders. Might as well take it now and get it over. He turned to face Steve.

"Yeah?"

Steve looked uncertain, almost embarrassed. "Uh . . . Gee, thanks."

Bart could not believe his ears. "Thanks?"

"Yeah. I guess you saved my life."

Bart's mouth hung open. Didn't the goon know that his

28

life would not have been in danger if Bart hadn't deliberately pulled him under?

"It was my fault that you went down, Steve. I pulled your legs out from under you."

Steve nodded. "Yeah. You didn't know. I can't swim."

Bart continued to stare, speechless. Steve knew what he had done, yet he thanked him!

4. TROUBLE AND MORE TROUBLE

BART HELPED HIMSELF TO MORE SALAD and potato chips and began on his fourth hot-dog. For some reason, it did not have quite the same marvelous flavor as the others. Could be he was no longer hungry!

The sun had dropped behind the mountains. The red afterglow painted the water an incredible rose color. The air, so warm all day, became quickly chill. The heat of the beach fire felt good on bare legs.

Conversation, which had slowed almost to a hush in the first—and even the second—round of hot-dogs, rose again to a loud incoherent babble, as the group which clustered around the beach fire began to eat more slowly.

"Another hot-dog, anybody?" called Lexy. No takers. Not even Steve, whose enormous appetite had not been dented by his ducking. "Well, then, how about some marshmallows?" She opened a big box and passed it around. Once more the gang surrounded the fire, holding toasting forks, each with a marshmallow impaled on its prongs, over the coals.

Bart quit after two of the golden-brown confections. There was a limit to a fellow's capacity, although you wouldn't think it to watch Steve still feeding his face after five or six hot-dogs.

The party was slowing down. He'd better do something to liven it up, Bart thought. He pushed his toasting fork in and out of the sand several times, to clean off the sticky goo. Then he held the long handled fork aloft and shouted, "How about a duel, somebody? On guard!"

"Oh, no, Bart!" cried Lexy quickly. "Not with forks! It's dangerous."

Bart stopped short. There he went again, starting something without thinking what might happen. A duel with those sharp-pronged toasting forks could end in serious injury. He thrust his fork into the sand, its point safely buried.

"I was only joking," he mumbled. He gathered up the rest of the discarded forks and parked them all together, out of harm's way.

But there was nothing against a harmless practical joke on Steve, who had just finished with his toasting fork and laid it aside. Steve was talking to Lexy and eating a marsh-mallow with his back turned. Bart took the other fellow's long-handled fork and with a stone pounded it into a log so that the prongs went deep in the wood.

When Steve turned around, Bart (and all the others who had observed the stunt) watched curiously. One big hand reached for another marshmallow. The other went out to the handle of the toasting fork—the only one in sight. An expression of surprise spread over Steve's face when the fork did not lift easily, as he had expected. His fingers closed tightly on the handle. He tugged. Nothing happened. Then he set his jaw, clutched the handle of the fork with both fists, and pulled hard.

The next instant Steve tumbled over backward against the pile of firewood, the handle of the fork in his big paws. The prongs remained embedded in wood.

Bart howled with mirth. Most of the others joined in. Steve grinned sheepishly as he got to his feet. Lexy, however, saw nothing funny in the incident. She avoided Bart's eyes.

The girls began to collect empty paper plates and cups and toss them on the fire. Lexy put the remains of the food on a tray and started to the house with it.

"Shall I throw some big chunks on the fire?" Bart asked her, still snickering at the memory of the look on Steve's face.

Lexy turned back. "What do you want to do, gang? Sit out here around the fire and sing and tell jokes? Or do you want to come in the house and dance?"

The boys were for staying on the beach, but the girls voted for dancing. Now that the sun had gone down, it was getting chilly down by the water, even with a fire, they said.

Bart started to ask Lexy if he should put out the fire, but she had already turned to Steve. "Put out the fire, will you, Steve?"

In disgust, Bart turned his back on the fire. If Lexy wanted that big jerk to take care of it, let him do it by

32

himself. He would make a botch of it, without a doubt. Probably didn't know any more about fires than he knew about fishing and swimming. But why should *he* care, Bart asked himself.

The Jensens' big recreation room made a swell place for dancing. There was room enough for all the whirls and fancy steps Bart liked to throw into any dance. He was a good dancer, he thought in satisfaction, as he piloted Polly around—light on his feet, good rhythm. And he was a good leader, too. Even though his partners, without exception, topped him by half a head or even a head, he could guide them over the floor easily and firmly. That was more than some of those skyscraper guys could do!

Yet tonight Lexy would not dance with him. Every time he sought her out, she said she had promised the dance to Steve. Was she just making excuses?

At each such disappointment Bart quickly found another partner, determined not to let Lexy know he cared how much she danced with Steve. He whirled and quick-stepped around the room in ever-increasing tempo. Let Lexy see what fun she was missing by sticking with old slowpoke, heavy-footed Steve.

The music stopped. Lexy and Steve went over to the phonograph to put on another record. Bart watched them out of the corner of his eye while he teased Polly about her red hair, pretending its brightness hurt his eyes.

Steve picked up a dozen records in one big paw. He selected one and put it on the record player. Then he set the rest of the stack back on the table and carelessly leaned his weight on them.

Cr-r-ack! It sounded like an explosion. Everybody turned to look. Steve lifted his hand from the records in consternation.

"What'd I do?" he asked stupidly.

Lexy examined the pile of records, one by one. Three on the bottom of the stack were broken. The back of an open album, making a ridge under the records, had caused the damage.

Steve apologized all over the place. "Gosh, I'm sorry," he kept saying. Lexy, like a good hostess, insisted it did not matter. But Bart knew her own allowance went into her records. This would hurt.

Yet Lexy cut short the profusion of Steve's halting apologies. "Forget it, Steve. You don't know your own strength."

Bart turned away. Women! You just couldn't figure them out. She wasn't mad at Steve at all, but for some reason (Bart could not imagine why) she acted as if she and Bart were no longer friends. The comradeship of the early afternoon had vanished completely with the beginning of the beach party.

As dancing started up again, someone mentioned the Freshman Hop, scheduled for a couple of months later. Bart's eyes lighted. The biggest dance of the freshman year —he would take Lexy to that. He would ask her tonight, before Steve got around to beating his time.

With this determination in mind, Bart dogged Lexy's steps. He made it a point to dance right behind her and her partner so that he would be on the spot when the dance ended. That way she would have to dance with him. She

34

couldn't have every dance promised.

Bart's strategy worked. Soon he had his arm around Lexy and was whirling her out on the floor.

For a minute they danced in silence. Lexy was not as light a dancer as Polly, but Bart would trade flighty, empty-headed Polly any day for her. Lexy was honest and sincere. You never wondered if she was laughing at you behind your back.

Bart summoned his courage and looked up at his partner. Better get this over before the record finished. "Will you go with me to the Freshman Hop, Lexy?"

Lexy frowned, not an angry frown, but an unhappy one. "I'm sorry, Bart."

He missed a step. "You mean you have a date already?"

"Well, no. Not exactly."

"Then what's the matter?"

Lexy hesitated. "I just don't want to, Bart."

"You want to go with Steve, I suppose." He had not meant to say it; it just popped out.

"Well, yes, if you must know. I do want to go with Steve."

Bart danced a moment in silence—no whirls, only straight dancing. After a few steps he asked, trying to keep his anxiety out of his voice, "Don't you like me any more?"

"Of course I like you."

"Don't you like to dance with me?"

"I like to dance with you *here* all right. But a big dance like the Freshman Hop . . . Everybody will be there, Bart."

He looked up at her, puzzled and hurt. Of course every-

35

body would be there. What difference did that make?

"Don't you understand, Bart?" Lexy asked earnestly. "I just don't like to be conspicuous."

Bart could not have been more hurt if she had slapped him in the face. So she did not like to go with a boy who was shorter than she! So she felt conspicuous when she danced with him! So she preferred Steve, clumsy, hulking Steve, who stepped on her toes and broke her records, just because he was big enough to tower over her!

Bart bent his head, pretending a need to watch his feet, but in reality to hide the moisture that scalded his eyes. To his unutterable relief, the music stopped. He dropped his arms and Lexy hurried over to the phonograph. Bart slipped quietly out of the room and headed for home, without even a goodnight or a courtesy "thank you." There was a limit to what a guy could take!

As he got ready for bed, Bart's mood became blacker than the night. Life was not worth living when you were the runt of the crowd. Maybe he should run away; go some place where people did not know how old he was, where he would not be compared with boys his own age but twice his size. But Bart knew he would not be happy playing and working with children of ten and eleven.

Eventually he drifted off into an uneasy sleep. He dreamed that he was a grown-up midget and the only job he could get was in the side-show of a circus. Lexy and Steve came to the circus and they stood and laughed at him, pointing him out to all the people who crowded around his cage.

Bart woke with a start, shaking uncontrollably. What a

*Bart could not have been more hurt . . . So she did not like
to go with a boy who was shorter than she!*

horrible dream! He flung the covers back and sat up in bed.

All of a sudden he became aware that something was wrong. The room, which should have been dark, glowed with an eerie light—not the soft pale yellow of moonlight, but a wild, flickering, ominous red light.

His personal troubles vanished. Bart leaped to the window and drew back the curtain. On the beach, a frightening sight met his eyes. Flames leaped and darted, smoke billowed and puffed. The whole beach was on fire!

Bart knocked frantically on his father's door. "The beach is on fire! Hurry, Dad!" Without waiting for an answer, he darted back to his own room to dress. Then he realized this fire was too big for garden hoses and amateur fire-fighters. He raced for the telephone in the hall to give the alarm.

As Bart pulled on slacks and shoes, he remembered the beach fire which Steve had been asked to put out. Without a doubt he had merely poured a little water on it, neglecting to scatter the embers first. And no one had checked to see if the coals were really dead. He himself, Bart thought guiltily, had never gone near it. Ordinarily, after a beach party, he checked the fire site the last thing before turning in, but last night he had been too perturbed to think of it.

Dr. Skinner had roused the Jensens and the neighbors between the two houses. The men, with the help of the young people, attached all available hose and began to spray water on the raging flames. It was like trying to stop the ocean tide. After a few minutes they gave up and stood, helpless and horrified, in the Jensens' yard.

38

"All the driftwood on the beach has caught," Dr. Skinner said. "If it once gets to that wooden bulkhead of yours . . ."

Mr. Jensen groaned. "I've been meaning for years to put in a cement bulkhead, like the rest of you people along here. I guess I'll have to, now. I won't have any bulkhead left."

39

Mrs. Skinner shrieked, "Look! Sparks on the roof!"

With one accord they turned all the hoses on the roofs of the three houses which stood closest to the holocaust. But the water fell short; extension ladders were needed, and longer hoses.

Suddenly Bart noticed a new sound over the threatening crackle of the fire. A thin high wail which grew louder and louder by the second. A siren! The fire engine was coming! Never in his life had Bart been so happy to hear that sound. Always before it had brought excitement and a little fear. This time it brought comfort and hope.

With a crescendo of sound, the fire engine tore down the street, stopping with a screech of brakes. The siren's shriek dwindled and died. Firemen swarmed down the driveway, carrying the heavy hose. A crowd began to gather, roused by the siren. In a few seconds a jet of water that even the hungry flames could not resist shot into the blazing beach and sent up a cloud of steam. Another hose soaked the roof and sides of every endangered house.

Minutes later, the fire was out. Bart and his father ventured near the bulkhead to survey the damage in the dim light of the half-moon. The old snag, which had been the back-log for so many beach parties, would never again perform that service. All the driftwood, for nearly two hundred feet of shore line, lay black and smoking. And the wooden bulkhead on Jensen's property, while not damaged enough to undermine it, was charred for over half its length. It would carry those scars for the remainder of its life, until Mr. Jensen replaced it with a cement wall.

The firemen loaded their equipment on the truck and

the engine rolled away. Slowly the crowd of neighbors dispersed.

"It was the beach party that started it, I suppose," Dr. Skinner said.

"Sure," Lexy's father answered. "Crazy, careless kids. Should have checked their fire myself, I guess. By the way, thanks for rousing us. If you hadn't seen the blaze when you did . . ."

Dr. Skinner threw his arm around Bart's shoulders. "Here is the fellow who gave the alarm. We all owe him a vote of thanks."

Bart flushed with pleasure. Feeling almost happy again, he followed his father back to the house and climbed into bed. At once he fell into a deep sleep, undisturbed by dreams of being a grown-up midget.

5. BART TURNS TEACHER

THE PERSISTENT JINGLING OF A HIGH-pitched bell roused Bart from a deep, dreamless sleep. What on earth was happening? Another fire? The telephone?

Only the alarm clock. Bart shut it off quickly. It was five o'clock Saturday morning. He had to get up and take Steve out fishing, as he had promised. Rats!

In the days that had passed since Lexy's beach party with its near-disaster aftermath, he had bounced back to his customary blithe behavior. Not that the hurt had healed; he still detested Steve, and he winced when he thought of Lexy's words. He avoided her as much as he could. No more saving a seat for her on the bus. No more phoning her to ask about lessons. No more dashing over to her house to borrow notebook paper, or see her biology notes. He just kept out of her way as much as possible, and out of Steve's way. Yet here he was, taking the fellow fishing!

Carrying his boots, Bart crept cautiously through the dark hall and into the kitchen. Now he could turn on a light without fear of waking anyone.

Why had he let himself in for this? Ordinarily Bart enjoyed getting up before dawn to fish, but that was when his companion was his father or Vic. Fishing with a fellow he did not like could be deadly.

Bart put on his mackinaw over his light-weight zipper jacket and pulled on his fishing cap and gloves. He gathered up his flashlight and the thermos of hot cocoa and the box of sandwiches his mother had prepared last night. Then he went softly down to the basement. His fishing gear, in a neat pile by the door, lay ready to stow in the boat.

It took two careful, quiet trips down to the beach to get the stuff into the skiff. Now for the motor. Bart started back to the house. A footstep on the driveway startled him. He flashed his light around. It was Steve.

Bart greeted him in a low voice. "Got your gear?"

Steve's answer rumbled like thunder through the dusk of approaching dawn. "Yeah, all I could rake up."

Bart shushed him angrily, "Pipe down," he warned in a low voice. "Want to wake the whole neighborhood?"

Steve muttered something in an apologetic tone and followed Bart into the basement.

Wham! What was that? Bart looked around quickly. Steve had stumbled over the can of extra gas. "Look where you're going," he cautioned in a furious whisper. "Take that can and the oars, and I'll carry the motor." The minute he had said it, Bart wished he had put it the other way around. He always found the heavy motor a clumsy burden, while husky Steve could handle it with no effort at all. But he would die rather than suggest it now.

43

He did not have to suggest it. Steve picked up the motor and started out with it, as if it weighed no more than a couple of books. "You hold the flashlight," he said in what was doubtless supposed to be a whisper. "I'll come back for the oars."

Five minutes later Bart stood on the beach and swept his light around, checking his preparations. Motor attached, extra gas, tackle box, rod and reel, net, oars, bait, lunch, bailing can, extra sheer pin in his pocket. Yes, they had everything.

Bart shoved the boat off the beach, and jumped in. He took up an oar and, standing in the boat, pushed gently but firmly against the gravelly bottom.

"There, I think we're deep enough now." After shipping the oar, Bart knelt in the stern of the boat and raised the head of the motor so that the propeller went down in the water.

"What can I do?" asked Steve.

"Take that oar and keep us off the beach. The tide is carrying us in again."

The sky had lightened considerably in the last few minutes. Glancing over his shoulder as he knelt before the engine, Bart saw Steve, a huge silhouette, poking awkwardly with an oar.

Bart forgot the need for quiet. "Hey! Take it easy!" he cried. "You'll break that oar." He scrambled to his feet. "This is the way." He took the oar out of Steve's clumsy hands and demonstrated the proper technique, firm but gentle, pulling the oar out of the water after each shove. "Now. You keep us from drifting while I start the motor."

44

Bart went back to his kneeling position in the stern of the boat. He wound the starter rope around the motor and pulled it with a firm, quick jerk. The engine started, coughed and died. Again he wound the rope. Again the motor failed to respond.

Over his shoulder he saw Steve laboring clumsily with the oar. At least he had not broken it yet, and he was keeping them off the beach.

At Bart's third attempt the engine faltered, then caught, and the boat sped through the water with a furious *put-put-put*. Bart grabbed the tiller and headed out to sea. With a sigh of relief, Steve dropped the oar and sank down on the middle seat.

"We'll step on it there, you goof!" Bart warned. "The oar! Lay it alongside the floorboards." Steve snatched at the oar. The blade caught on a rib of the boat. There was a splintering snap, and Steve looked down, chagrined, at the split blade.

Bart raged. "Now you've done it! What if the motor conks out, clumsy?"

"Gosh, Bart! I'm sorry!"

Bart paid no attention to Steve's attempted apology. "Of all the dumb stunts! Haven't you any sense at all? I might have known you'd wreck everything." Bart fairly sputtered in his rage.

"I didn't mean . . ." There was no doubting the contrition in the big fellow's voice. Bart bit his lip. Oh, well, no use bawling Steve out any more. The guy really did not know how strong he was.

"Okay. Forget it." But his tone indicated plainly that

Bart himself had no intention of forgetting the incident.

The boat sped on through the cold dawn. Bart looked back at his own house, dark and silent against the pale sky. It was going to be a nice day.

They were approaching the lighthouse now. Bart cut the motor's speed as low as it would go, for trolling. "This is the best place to fish, off this point." His voice was calm again; he would be a good sport this morning if it killed him, no matter how many fool stunts Steve pulled. "Better start rigging your line."

It was light enough now to see clearly. Pausing occasionally to bring the boat back on course with a touch of the tiller, Bart attached sinker, leader, dodger and hooks to his line with swift, expert fingers. Then he extracted a herring from his packet of frozen bait and threaded it onto the hooks. With the speed and surety born of experience, he dropped his baited hooks gently into the water and paid out line until he judged he had the right amount. Then he propped his rod against the gunwale of the boat and turned to see how Steve was progressing.

Why, the fellow did not even have his leader on yet!

"What's the trouble?"

"I'm all thumbs," Steve confessed, grinning foolishly. "How do you tie this thing, anyway?"

Bart reached for the line. "Here, I'll show you. Didn't your dad ever teach you to rig a line?"

"No." Steve's voice had a queer note. "My . . . dad hasn't taught me very much . . . yet."

A few quick movements and the job was done. "There."

"It looks easy when you do it." Steve looked at his tackle

46

doubtfully. "Now what do I do?"

"Lead sinker. About eight ounces. That leader is too long. Three feet is enough." Bart cut the leader with his pocketknife and selected a sinker from Steve's box. "This the biggest you have?"

"I don't know," Steve acknowledged. "I borrowed this stuff from my father's brother."

"Your father's brother? He's your uncle, isn't he?"

"I guess you'd call him that."

Why, the dumb cluck! How stupid could you get? Didn't know his father's brother was bound to be his uncle! Well, one thing was certain: Steve would never make a fisherman. You had to be smarter than the fish to catch them, and Steve would never outwit even a clam!

As Bart's fingers worked deftly, he explained every move to the big fellow opposite him. "You want your bait up pretty close to your dodger. The herring mustn't turn over; it must whip from side to side, so it looks like a live fish. There. Now you are ready."

Steve took the rod in one hand and the leader in the other. "Do I just throw it in?"

"No, you dope! Drop it in easy, and pay out line slowly so your sinker won't catch up to your bait and foul it up."

Steve looked bewildered. He made no move to put his line into the water.

"Go on." Bart spoke irritably. "Pay out about forty or fifty feet of line."

"How can I tell how much I put out?"

"Count your pulls. You'll put out about a yard at a time."

Slowly, carefully, Steve let out the necessary amount of

47

line. "Now what?"

"Set your drag."

Steve stared at his instructor, bewildered.

"Look." Bart tried very hard to be patient. He indicated the gadget on the reel. "The friction disk is like a clutch that squeezes up on the line. You want a little friction, but you don't want it too tight." Bart adjusted the disk. "Here, feel this as you pull the line." Steve did as Bart directed. "That's about the way it should feel when it is properly adjusted. Too loose, and your line goes out too fast. Too tight, and there is not enough play, your line might break when a fish strikes."

Steve nodded, his thumb on the line. A broad smile spread over his big face. "Yeah, I feel it."

"Okay." Bart was beginning to enjoy his role of teacher. Steve might be dumb, but he certainly appreciated instruction.

For a few minutes both boys sat quietly, watching their lines at intervals. Bart increased the speed of the motor slightly, then after a few seconds slowed it down again. "Makes the lure seem more like a live fish when the speed changes. One way to fool the salmon," he explained.

Streaks of pink showed in the eastern sky now. A breeze sprang up, brushing the water into tiny waves. Bart pulled the collar of his mackinaw higher around his neck. Maybe they should have some cocoa. He turned the tiller a trifle, then reached for the thermos.

As he unscrewed the thermos lid, he pointed out to his big student the rhythmic jerk of the tip of his rod. "See how the tip of your pole acts?"

48

"Yeah. Why is that?"

"The action of the bait. It means the flasher is working right. When your pole stops moving like that, or the action changes, something is wrong. Have some cocoa?"

"Gosh! I never thought to bring anything to eat." Steve accepted cocoa and a sandwich gratefully, holding his rod between his knees.

"Always goes good, out on the water like this," Bart answered with his mouth full. "The salt air makes you hungry."

"I'm hungry all the time," Steve confessed, reaching for another sandwich. "Mrs. Huber . . . my mother, I mean . . . says I never get filled up."

Bart raised his eyebrows. He'd never heard of a kid calling his mother "Mrs." He checked the tiller again, and glanced at both rods. "Better reel in, Steve. Check your bait. Something is haywire."

The big fellow turned the crank slowly and awkwardly. Bart reached out for the leader when the bait appeared and brought it into the boat.

"A silver hit it," he announced after a glance at the herring.

"How do you know?" Steve asked curiously.

"Just raked it with his teeth. A dog fish would have taken chunks out." Bart settled the bait on the hooks more securely and Steve put the line back in the water. Bart was glad to notice that the other fellow remembered to measure the line as he put it out, and to let it out slowly enough so that the leader would ride clear. Maybe Steve was not so dumb, after all. Maybe he was just ignorant.

49

The boys finished the sandwiches and cocoa and wished for more. Bart reeled in his line, checked his bait, and put it out again.

An hour passed. They weren't the only fishermen out this morning: other boats appeared, specks in the distance. Bart turned the skiff in a wide circle, and steered past the lighthouse again. Across the bay, a ferry caught the light of the rising sun and glinted like a silver salmon.

"What's a fishing derby?" Steve asked suddenly.

Bart could not believe his ears. "What?"

"This Kids' Fishing Derby I see advertised—what is it?"

"You mean you really don't know?"

Steve shook his head and smiled his silly smile. "Never heard of such a thing before."

Bart looked at him incredulously. "Never heard of a fishing derby? Where have you been all your life?"

It seemed to Bart that Steve hesitated before answering. "Sacramento."

"Oh!" Bart wondered if people in Sacramento did not fish. "A fishing derby is sort of a race, a contest. They try to see who can catch the biggest fish in a certain time. Some derbies last for weeks and others for days. In most of them you have to catch a certain size fish to qualify. The Harbor City Kids' Fishing Derby lasts only four hours, from six in the morning till ten. We don't have any qualifying rounds."

"Can anybody in Harbor City enter?"

"Anybody who is over ten and under fifteen. I've been in three derbies already."

50

Steve looked at his line thoughtfully. "Under fifteen, huh?"

"That's the rule."

"Then this will be my only chance. I'll be fifteen before it comes around again."

Bart nodded. "I've got one more year to go after this. I'm not fourteen yet."

All of a sudden Steve cried, "Look at my pole!"

Quickly Bart turned to look, then he moved the tiller sharply to the left. "You've got a strike! No, don't try to reel in! Give him all the line he wants."

Bart snatched his own rod and began to crank hurriedly. In spite of his excitement, Steve noticed his companion's actions.

"Have you got one, too?"

"No, I'm taking in my line so your fish won't get fouled up in it. A fisherman always hauls in when someone near him hooks a fish."

His gear safely in the boat, Bart turned his attention to the tiller. He concentrated on following the speeding fish.

"Criminy!" Steve was breathless with excitement. "How far is he going?"

"He's trying to get away, but we'll follow him."

Minutes passed. Steve's reel continued to zing as the line ran out. Then all action stopped.

"Try reeling in now," Bart advised. "But take it easy. If he starts going again, give him his head, but tighten your drag a little more." He slowed the motor.

Cautiously, big hands trembling, Steve reeled in. One

turn . . . two . . . ten . . . twenty . . . Still no motion from the fish. Suddenly Steve's pole bent almost double.

"Let him go!" yelled Bart.

Steve did as he was told, and the line began to unwind again.

"He's off again," Bart said. He speeded up the engine and the boat followed the fish.

At last the salmon seemed exhausted. He let Steve bring him up close to the boat. Bart, net in hand, leaned over the side. "Just a little closer, Steve. But be ready in case he decides to make another run." Carefully Bart bent over and got the net under the nearly exhausted fish. "There! We've got him!"

Steve gazed down in awe at the beautiful salmon threshing around on the bottom of the boat. "I never thought I'd do it! I never thought I'd do it!"

As he gave the salmon a quick sharp merciful blow on the head, Bart thought privately that Steve never would have landed it if it hadn't been for his own help, but he merely said, "It's a beauty. Must weigh close to ten pounds."

Both boys baited up and let their lines out again. The breeze picked up. The sun burst into view over the lighthouse. Across the bay, the mountains reflected back the rosy light. Bart drew a deep breath. He loved it out on the Sound like this, in the early morning. He was glad now that he had let himself be trapped into taking Steve fishing. It had not been so bad, after all. Steve wasn't half as stupid as he had thought.

Just then Bart's rod bent way over. He snatched it from the boat and shouted to Steve, "Reel in, fast! I've got a strike."

For a few seconds Bart was too busy to notice whether Steve obeyed or not. This fish was really a live one, a get-away-or-die salmon. Must be a big one.

The tension of the line eased suddenly. Bart started to crank cautiously; then, realizing that the fish had doubled back and was making for the boat, he began to crank frantically. At the same time he saw that Steve had made no move to reel in; but merely sat, wide-eyed, watching. He had not even taken up his rod!

"Reel in, I tell you!" shrieked Bart. "He's coming this way. He'll tangle with your line, sure."

At last Steve got into action. He grabbed his pole and started to crank with more energy than care. But it was too late. Bart saw his salmon—a fine big one—making straight for the skiff. He went underneath it, barely missing the propeller, and then Bart's line went slack.

Bart knew what had happened before he saw the empty leader dangling at the end of his line.

He turned furiously to Steve, who was looking blankly at his own broken line. "You fouled my line! I'd have had him if you'd reeled in when you should."

Steve grinned foolishly. "Gosh, I'm sorry, Bart."

"Sorry!" fumed Bart. "Of all the stupid, dumb, idiotic dimwits I ever saw, you're the worst. Dead from the neck up. You . . . you dope!"

Steve waited until he simmered down. Then he said humbly, "I'm awfully sorry, Bart. I didn't mean to."

Bart sat down and opened his tackle box, trying to control his anger. That's what he got for taking a novice like

Steve out fishing. Didn't know the first thing about the rules of the game. You'd think anybody would have more sense than that. How come he had never learned to fish?

Without another word, Bart rigged his line again, but he made no move to help Steve, although he watched the latter's bungling efforts out of the corner of his eye. Bart had his line in the water a good five minutes before Steve finally launched his.

They fished in silence for another hour, without even a nibble. At last Bart turned the boat around and headed home.

"We can troll until we get in," he said, breaking the long silence, "but I doubt that we'll catch anything now."

The motor sputtered. "If it conks out," Bart cast a dark look at the broken oar, "we'll have to swim in and tow the boat."

Steve gave him a startled glance. Then Bart remembered; Steve could not swim. "We'll just have to wait for the Coast Guard to pick us up," he amended. "We might have to wait for days," he added, enjoying Steve's look of dismay.

But the motor did not die. It resumed its rhythmic put-put. Bart brought the boat back on course and steered the rest of the way in silence.

When the boat had been safely beached and everything put away, Steve took up his precious fish, his borrowed tackle and the broken oar.

"I know you think I'm stupid, Bart, and . . . Well, I'm sorry about the oar . . . and your fish."

"Forget it," Bart answered gruffly.

"Well . . ." Steve scuffed the cement with his huge

shoe. "I sure thank you, Bart. I've been wanting to learn how to fish."

Bart looked up at him sharply. "How come this sudden interest in fishing, Steve? How come you're so anxious to learn to fish?"

Steve grinned his sheepish grin. "I want to enter the Kids' Fishing Derby. I'd like to win that bike."

Bart stared after Steve's big figure, taking long strides up the driveway. "Well, how do you like that!" he whispered incredulously to himself. "He gets me to teach him to fish so he can beat me in the Derby!"

Then the memory of Steve's clumsiness returned to him and Bart began to laugh. Fat chance Steve had of winning any Fishing Derby!

6. ECKLUND'S ISLAND

IT WAS A BUSY SATURDAY FOR BART. After Steve left, he went into the house for a man-sized breakfast. Then he raced through his week-end chores to be ready in time for the overnight boat trip which had been planned long before the fishing session with Steve had materialized. As a farewell fling to summer, Parker, a classmate of Bart's, had planned an overnight trip to Ecklund's Island. Parker's father (Harbor City's millionaire lumberman) had agreed to let his son take their sixteen-foot runabout, with 25-horse outboard motor, and Parker had invited Bart and Vic and Al to go along.

Loaded down with his packsack of food, his fishing gear, and his sleeping bag with a change of clothing and a flashlight rolled inside, plus a few little things he intended to have fun with, Bart staggered down the beach to Parker's palatial home, which was one of the show places of Harbor City. The runabout, the *Ginger II*, lay out in the bay, anchored to her buoy. Parker and Vic were loading a pile

56

of gear into the dinghy at the water's edge, but there was no sign of Al.

Vic waved cheerfully to Bart, but Parker scarcely looked up from his work. "Don't put that stuff in here," he warned, as Bart started to pile his things in the little boat. "This dinghy is too small for such a load. I'll take Vic out to the *Ginger*, then I'll come back for you and Steve."

"Steve!" Bart's voice expressed the dismay he felt. Surely Steve wasn't going on this trip! "I thought Al was going?"

Parker settled down to rowing, and Vic answered the question, calling across the widening gap of water. "Al can't come. His mother's sick and he can't leave her alone, so he asked Steve to buy him out."

That made sense. Each guest had agreed to bring food for one meal, and after paying out hard cash for bacon and eggs and stuff, Al would try to get his money back some way. But why Steve, of all people?

Heavy footsteps along the bulkhead announced the approach of an elephant—or Steve.

It was Steve, of course. Bart turned his back to hide his scowl. After fishing with the dope half the morning, now he had to put up with him the rest of the day, and tomorrow, too.

"Hi, Bart!" Steve sounded pleased with himself. "Sure is nice of you guys to let me go with you."

"It's Parker's boat," Bart answered grudgingly. "He has the say-so."

"Yeah." Steve tossed his sleeping bag down to the beach. Then he set the rest of his load on the sea wall and jumped down on the beach himself. He lifted down his box of food as lightly as if it were empty, and turned to grin again at Bart, oblivious of the latter's thunderous frown.

"Sure a break for me that Al couldn't go. I didn't know, this morning when we were fishing, that I'd be seeing you this afternoon."

"I didn't know it, either," Bart thought grimly, "or I sure wouldn't have gone out with you this morning."

"Hi-ya, Steve!" Parker was back with the dinghy. Vic had stayed on board the cruiser. "Get in, Bart. I'll come back for you, Steve."

All the way out to the *Ginger II* Bart sat glum and silent. But when Parker had shoved off for his return trip to get his other passenger, Bart blew up.

"Whose idea was it to ask Steve," he sputtered to Vic. "I thought this was supposed to be a trip for *fun*."

Vic's slow, tolerant smile did nothing to calm Bart's anger. "I guess it was Al's idea. Anyway, he asked Parker . . ."

"Rats! He should have let us choose, too. It's a dirty trick!"

Vic's grin widened. "Keep your shirt on," he advised gently. "It's Parker's boat. He's the one to say who can go."

Bart knew Vic was right, but he wasn't going to admit it. The memory of Steve's clumsiness and stupidity (the broken oar and the fish that got away, Lexy's smashed records and the fire that was not put out) filled him with a gloomy certainty that the trip would be utterly spoiled.

"If I hadn't spent all that money on this grub for dinner tonight," he muttered darkly, kicking his packsack, "I'd pull out right now and go on home."

58

Vic finished stowing the sleeping bags under the cowl and sat down, stretching out his skinny legs. "Oh, come off it, Bart. Steve's all right."

Bart snorted. Vic thought everybody was all right. There was no use arguing with him, however; he would never listen to anything against his friends—but since when was Steve a friend of Vic's? Bart had thought his pal had little in common with gawky Steve.

Before Bart could say anything more, the dinghy was back. The other two boys climbed aboard the cruiser, and Bart forgot his anger in the excitement and confusion of getting under way. Even when he stumbled over Steve's big feet, going forward after helping Parker to tie the rowboat up to the buoy and cast off the *Ginger II*, Bart felt only momentary irritation. This trip would be the last one of the season, before the autumn storms set in, and he meant to enjoy it thoroughly, in spite of Steve.

The motor started smoothly; Bart wished he had one of those self-starters for his motor. The boat skimmed through the water, leaving a beautiful wake behind her. The sun glinted on the windshield and the polished mahogany decking; Bart wished he had a runabout like this, instead of his battered old skiff.

Parker settled down behind the wheel; Bart wished Parker would let him steer, but he wasn't going to suggest it. He drew a deep breath of the sharp salt air. "Ecklund's Island, here we come!" he shouted.

"How far is it to this island?" asked Steve.

The other three answered at once, each giving a different estimate. They all laughed.

59

"With this boat, we could make it in an hour," Parker summed it up, "but we'll stop to troll after a while."

"I don't think I've ever been there," Steve observed.

"Probably not," Vic agreed. "No ferries stop there. No reason why they should. There's nothing there any more."

"Except ghosts," Bart amended.

"Ghosts?" Steve repeated.

"Yeah. Old Man Ecklund and his son. They just disappeared."

Parker nodded. "Left their beautiful sloop riding at anchor. Left their big house with all the furnishings, even their clothes and food."

There was silence for a few minutes, while the graceful boat skimmed lightly through the water. They passed a tremendous log boom, pulled by a dirty looking tugboat that inched its way down the bay so slowly it seemed scarcely to leave a wake. Parker tooted his whistle at the tug and the hardworking tugboat tooted back.

"One of my father's log booms," Parker explained.

"But what happened to old man Ecklund?" Steve asked at last.

"Nobody knows," Vic answered. "He never turned up. Never was seen again."

"But plenty of people have *heard* him," Bart put in.

"Heard him?" Steve repeated.

"Ecklund's ghost. We'll probably hear it tonight." Bart noted with delight Steve's involuntary shiver.

Vic laughed tolerantly. "Just one of those stories that gets going around, like any haunted house story."

"You'll see," Bart prophesied darkly. "Just wait and see."

60

He fingered the water whistle he had tucked in his jacket pocket. Yes, it was there, all right. Bart smiled to himself. He would have some fun later on.

A small freighter, one of the fleet that plied between the various Puget Sound ports, cut across their bow. Parker gave his whistle signal and waved, receiving an answering salute from the freighter.

"My dad owns a half interest in that company," Parker said. "All the skippers know me."

He cut the motor to low speed. "We'll troll for a while,"

61

he announced, reaching for his fishing gear. In a few seconds Vic, Bart and Parker each had a line out.

Steve watched them ruefully. "I never thought to bring any stuff for fishing." Then his face brightened. "But I caught a dandy this morning, didn't I, Bart? Mrs.—my mother—said she would wait to cook it until I got back. She put it in the refrigerator."

"I hope you cleaned it first," Bart said.

"Cleaned it?"

"For heavens sake! Don't you know how to clean a fish?"

Steve shook his head. Bart burst into a mocking laugh. "Brother! That will be some tasty salmon by the time your mother cooks it!"

All the light drained out of Steve's face. Obviously he had really been looking forward to that salmon dinner.

Vic came to the rescue. "Don't you worry, Steve. Your mother or your father will surely clean it."

"Do you think so?" Steve's voice was pathetically eager.

"Sure."

Steve sighed with relief. Bart, annoyed at Vic's quick move to reassure the big lunk, couldn't help noticing how Steve never thought to question Vic's word. Why was it people always trusted Vic, when they were very slow indeed to believe Bart? It wasn't fair.

Several airplanes had passed overhead, without rating even a glance from the boys; there was so much aircraft building in the Northwest that planes were as common as mosquitoes in a swamp. But now a different kind of aircraft drew their attention.

"Look at the helicopter," said Vic. "Navy, isn't it?"

Parker looked up, shading his eyes. Then he tooted his whistle and waved. The helicopter ducked in a salute.

"I suppose that belongs to your dad, too," Bart observed caustically.

"Not exactly." Parker did not seem to get the implied sarcasm. "The guy who operates that helicopter is a friend of Dad's. He has promised me a ride in it one of these days."

Bart seethed. What a snob Parker was! Just because his father had made a fortune in the lumber business, he thought he owned the earth. He ought to be taken down a peg or two.

"Wake up, Bart. You've got a strike." Vic's words roused him to action. But either he was too late, or the fish had not really taken the bait, for his line went slack immediately. Bart reeled in, annoyed at himself for losing the fish.

Then Parker reeled in, too, for Vic had a strike.

Vic's fish was a small salmon trout, weighing a couple of pounds, possibly. A little later Parker caught one too, slightly larger than Vic's. From the way he beamed, you would have thought it was a mammoth king salmon.

At once Parker announced that they were through trolling now, and he speeded up the motor.

"How about me?" Bart protested. "Aren't you going to give me a chance to catch a fish, too?"

"Sorry." Parker looked anything but sorry. "We want to get ashore and set up camp before dark."

Bart snorted. The sun was still an hour above the horizon. But he could see that Parker had no intention of letting him troll any longer, so he put up his fishing tackle, feeling like a martyr.

As they approached Ecklund's Island, Bart forgot his irritation with Parker and Steve in the never-failing appeal of this small isolated island. Part of its charm lay in its history, he knew: in the mystery that surrounded its early inhabitants. But part of it was the beauty of the island, itself: the rocky cliff straight ahead that dropped sheer to the water, the wooded hill to the right with its gentle slope to the beach, the row of old piling, which was all that remained of the dock.

Parker had slowed the motor. "Want to cruise around the island before we land?" he asked.

The others agreed immediately.

"Let me steer a while, Parker." Bart was surprised to find himself saying it. He had wanted to get hold of that shiny big wheel from the time they started, but pride had kept him from asking, if Parker would not offer. Now the words had come out of their own accord.

Parker shook his head. "My dad said not to trust anybody else with this boat. She cost a lot of money, you know."

Bart flushed. Parker talked as if he, Bart, did not know how to handle a boat. Why, he knew more about motors and boats than Parker ever would! He had handled a motorboat since he was nine. But if Parker wanted to be selfish, who cared? Certainly Bart would never give him the satisfaction of knowing that he minded in the least. He pretended to be very busy searching the shore with his eyes.

Parker selected the sandy beach by the old wharf for his landing spot. He ran the boat in as close as he could. Then the other three, shedding their shoes and socks, and rolling up their pants, jumped into the water ankle deep and pulled

64

the boat half out of the water. Minutes later, they had the cruiser unloaded, and had dragged it up on the beach, well above the high tide mark.

"That ought to do," observed Parker, lifting out the anchor and wedging it between two big logs. "We'll spread our sleeping bags out along here and build our fire over there."

For a little while the boys worked busily. Vic and Steve chopped wood. Parker cleared a space for the sleeping bags. Bart cleaned the two salmon the others had caught and went to the little creek for water. While he was there, he filled his water whistle and put it back in his pocket.

At last everything was ready; the sleeping bags were laid out, the fire ready to light, the kettle for tea hung over it on a forked stick.

"Let's explore before we start supper," Vic suggested.

Bart picked up his flashlight. "Sure. Let's show Steve old Ecklund's dungeon."

Bart had seen the ruined remains of the old estate many times, but the place always fascinated him. Nothing remained of the house but the foundation and the floor, some broken glass and a few bricks. Generations of campers had long since burned all of the fallen timbers.

But the "dungeon" itself had changed little with the years. "My dad says this was really just a cellar, not a dungeon at all," Parker said as the boys climbed down the rough stone steps into the airless room.

Bart swept his light around the damp earth floor, the stone walls and the heavy beams overhead. It really did look like a dungeon.

"I'll bet Old Man Ecklund buried his money here," Vic said. "They say he had plenty, and he didn't believe in banks."

"You really think so?" asked Steve. "Why don't we dig and see if we can find it."

Bart laughed, and the sound echoed weirdly in the cellar. "More likely he was buried here himself, and that's why his ghost hangs around."

Suddenly Bart's flashlight went out. Silently he ducked back to the steps. At once a gurgling, moaning whistle rose in the damp cold air, and died away gradually in the darkness.

7. THE GHOST

FOR A FEW SECONDS THE "DUNGEON" WAS dark and silent, except for the sound of quick breathing. Then Vic laughed.

"I thought ghosts always waited until night to do their stuff," he observed cheerfully. "Hey, Bart, what happened to your flashlight?"

Bart moved softly to the center of the cellar. "Might have had a loose connection," he said smoothly, turning the switch back on. "There. It's all right now."

With one accord, the boys climbed up the rough steps to the fresh outdoors and the daylight. They went on up the hill to the old neglected orchard. No one mentioned the ghost.

At last Bart asked, "Do you suppose it really was a ghost?"

Parker denied it with more vehemence than was necessary. "Of course not! Who ever heard of such a thing? Only ignorant people believe in ghosts."

Steve took it up. "Sure. I never did believe in ghosts."

Bart smiled secretly. He had heard the others breathing hard, down there in the "dungeon." "Weren't you scared at all?" he asked, pretending surprise and admiration.

Parker and Steve were loud in their denials. Vic said not a word. Bart smiled again, and then changed the subject. "Better fill your pockets with these apples," he said, pointing to the gnarled old trees half hidden in brush, still bearing small, misshapen fruit. "The only dessert I brought for dinner is cookies."

For an hour the boys roamed the small island, climbing trees and cliffs, exploring trails and thickets. Then everybody except Steve went swimming. No matter how they coaxed, they could not get the big fellow into the water.

"Aren't you ever going to learn to swim?" Bart taunted.

Steve flushed. "I'll try tomorrow," he promised.

When the boys returned to the camp site after their swim, they were all absolutely ravenous. Bart, as cook for the evening meal, produced wieners and opened canned spaghetti. But the boys were so hungry they would not wait for anything to be properly cooked. When Bart started to put the salmon in the frying pan, a howl went up.

"We can't wait for these to cook!" yelped Steve.

"Save them for a midnight snack," Parker advised, and the others agreed.

The spaghetti was eaten lukewarm, and the wieners practically raw. Two loaves of bread and half a pound of butter disappeared like magic, washed down by quarts of tea.

Not until every bite of this food had been cleaned up did Bart remember the raw carrots which were to have been the vegetable and salad combined. But nobody minded the

Then everybody except Steve went swimming. No matter how they coaxed, they could not get the big fellow into the water.

oversight. The carrots were munched, along with cookies and apples, as dessert.

While Bart washed the tin plates and cups and forks, and scoured the spaghetti kettle with sand, the others lolled around the fire, which they had built up as much for light as for heat. The sun had long since set, and the rosy afterglow faded fast. Bart whistled softly as he rinsed the dishes and stacked them beside the fire to dry. Funny: he didn't mind doing dishes and cooking on a camping trip, but he hated them at home.

The boys had begun to argue about their relative speed and strength. Soon they were all four embroiled in a series of races, grip challenges, hand stands, wrestling, and so on. This impromptu track meet continued until everybody was tired out—even Steve—and all dropped down in the sand by the fire to catch their breath.

Bart was very near exhaustion. Before dinner, he had dived and swum twice as much as anyone else, and after dinner he had taken part in every one of the speed and strength trials, wrestling and all—although everybody knew he did not stand a chance against Parker and Steve in feats of strength.

In speed and agility, however, he had shown them all up. He had beaten them in straight racing, and in cartwheels and hand stands. He could still hear the exclamations of admiration at his balancing feats, and they were music to his ears. Maybe he wasn't a big strong-arm guy, but there were some fields in which he could beat them all.

Finally Vic rose to his feet, announcing, "If we're going to have those salmon for a late supper, we'd better get them

in the fire." He wrapped the fish in kelp. Then he raked the coals away from one side of the fire, laid the sea-weed bundle on the hot sand, covered it with more sand, and then raked glowing coals over the top.

"They ought to be ready by the time we're hungry again," he said, getting to his feet and brushing the sand from his hands.

"I'm hungry again now," declared Steve.

Vic laughed. "I'll bet you could almost keep up with Paul

71

Bunyan when it comes to eating," he said, pushing a log farther into the fire.

"Who is this Paul Bunyan I hear so much about?" asked Steve. "I don't think I've met him."

The others roared with delight. Vic explained that Paul Bunyan is the favorite mythical character of the Northwest, the hero of a hundred tall tales. He told how Paul Bunyan and his Blue Ox, Babe, dug Puget Sound for Old Man Puget, but started to fill it in again when his employer failed to keep his bargain about pay.

"This island we're on," Vic finished in his slow drawl, "is nothing but one of the spadefuls of dirt that Paul Bunyan tossed back into the big ditch he had dug. When Old Man Puget saw that he meant to fill in the whole ditch, he paid him what he owed him right fast. But Paul had already tossed in several hundred spadefuls of dirt, and those are the islands in the Sound."

One Paul Bunyan story led to another, with Parker and Bart contributing their full share. They told about the year of the blue snow, about the popcorn freeze, about the mile-square kitchen griddle, and all the other tall tales that have delighted many generations of listeners. And Steve was a very satisfactory audience, going into gales of laughter at each new absurdity.

Suddenly Parker, in the middle of a story, stopped short, staring down the beach into the darkness.

"What's the matter, Park?" asked Vic.

Parker gulped twice before he replied. "Look!"

The others followed the direction of his pointing finger, and shivered at the eerie sight that met their eyes. Down

72

toward the water's edge (in the moonless night it was impossible to tell just how far in the tide had come) two big balls of fire floated in the air!

"There *is* a ghost here!" whispered Steve in awe.

In spite of himself, Bart gulped nervously. He knew there must be some natural explanation, but for the life of him he could not think of one. The circles were probably the eyes of some animal, but what animal? A cat's eyes would be smaller and much closer to the ground . . . and anyway, there were no cats or dogs on the island. There were no deer or elk, either, and he had never seen any signs of bear around here.

Nobody moved. All eyes were riveted on those balls of light.

All of a sudden, they disappeared. The light just went out, as if someone had blown out a candle.

The boys watched for a few seconds, tense. Just as they began to relax, the weird lights reappeared. Then a small, sharp sound sifted through the darkness, a cracking sound.

At once Bart smiled and relaxed. He knew, now, what it was, down there at the edge of the water. He reached for the flashlight.

"I'll go down and find out what it is," he offered, getting quietly to his feet.

Steve looked at him open-mouthed. "You're not afraid?"

"Afraid? What is there to be afraid of? You said yourself there's no such thing as ghosts."

Vic looked at his friend shrewdly. "Is this one of your tricks, Bart?"

In the glow of the fire, Bart's face was all innocence.

73

"Tricks? What are you talking about?"

"Water whistles," Vic answered dryly. "And flashlight switches."

Bart grinned. He hadn't taken Vic in for a minute on that ghost stunt. But the others had fallen for it. "On my honor," he said, "there's no trick about this."

He kicked off his shoes and circled stealthily around to the right of the mysterious eyes. His bare feet made no noise, and not a sound came from the group by the fire.

Again the circles of light vanished, then reappeared in a few seconds. Again the boys heard that sharp, cracking sound.

Bart had almost reached the water now. He could hear the whisper of the gentle swells as they rolled over the sand and fell back.

The balls of fire were quite close to him now. He decided he could not risk trying to get any nearer. He stood where he was and pointed his flashlight at the disembodied eyes. Then he pushed the switch, and the group at the fire burst out laughing.

The beam of light from the powerful flashlight revealed a startled raccoon, sitting on his hind legs, eating a late dinner of clams! Instantly, surprised and indignant, he dropped to all four feet and scooted away in the darkness. The boys howled with mirth.

Bart swaggered back to the campfire, enjoying the amazement and amusement of the others. They bombarded him with questions.

"Did you know all the time what it was?"

"How did you know it wasn't a ghost?"

"What if it had been a bear?"

74

Bart relished the imputation of bravery so much he did not disclose the reasoning which led him to the correct solution of the mystery. He did not reveal that it was the cracking noise which had reminded him of the raccoon's habit of digging clams at low tide and washing and cracking them on the spot for a nocturnal meal.

Soon Vic decided it was about time for their midnight snack. With a long stick he raked the coals off the salmon. The kelp had scorched to a crisp, and the skin of the fish looked charred.

"Gosh!" exclaimed Steve regretfully. "It's spoiled, isn't it?"

Vic merely grinned and divided the fish into four equal portions. How surprised Steve looked when he found that underneath that unappetizing skin, the flesh was pink and tender and delicious. The boys made short work of the two small salmon and wished for more.

They climbed into their sleeping bags at last. Steve looked up at the starless sky and spoke doubtfully. "What'll we do, without any tent, if it rains?"

"Crawl inside your sleeping bag," Vic advised.

"Wouldn't I smother?" Steve asked.

"Probably," Bart replied cheerfully. "But they say it's such a nice painless death, you wouldn't mind."

Steve joined good-naturedly in the laugh that followed.

Although the boys were very tired, no one showed any disposition to go to sleep. The fire had died low, and the moon had risen, before they finally stopped talking and drifted off to sleep, lulled by the lapping of the incoming tide.

8. GOEDUCKS AND PSEUDO-GOEDUCKS

BART WOKE WITH THE FIRST GRAY LIGHT of dawn, his head wet and cold with dew. Vic and Parker had crawled down into their sleeping bags, and Steve had rolled over a couple of times, apparently, sleeping bag and all, for his face was in the cold ashes of last night's fire. As Bart watched, the big fellow stirred and rolled again. Bart chuckled softly. Steve would never get that black off his face in cold salt water.

The tide was out, way out. The beach seemed to stretch for blocks before it met the dark gray water. This must be one of the lowest tides of the season.

Bart climbed quietly out of his sleeping bag and put on his shoes and his jacket. He shivered. The air was chilly this morning. Quickly he gathered some wood and some bark and made a fire. He had a little trouble getting it going, for everything was dew-soaked, but at last a feeble blaze flickered and sputtered. Bart put his head down to the side of the fire and blew gently, until the blaze gathered strength

76

At a minus tide you could see things that were ordinarily
covered from human eyes—like that sea anemone . . .

enough to fight by itself against the wet wood.

Then he got to his feet and walked down the beach toward the water.

Low tide was always interesting. At a minus tide you could see things that were ordinarily covered from human eyes—like that sea anemone that looked like a flower, but was really an animal. When you touched it all the beautiful flower-like appendages disappeared. Then there was the moon snail, leaving its shiny track. And the starfish, all sizes, from an inch or so in diameter to a foot or more, all gorgeous colors. And plenty of barnacles, of course, in their geometric limestone houses. And tiny crabs and cockles. . . .

Clams spurted all around him as he walked. Bart toyed with the idea of digging a mess of tender little butter clams for breakfast, but discarded it. He doubted that the fellows would care for shellfish for breakfast; they were much better as a lunch or dinner or supper dish. And anyway, it was Steve's turn to cook the meal. Let him do the work.

Now Bart saw the big necks of some tough old horse clams sticking up through the sand. Each one spouted a stream of water into the air. Bart made a face. Horse clams! The least appetizing of all the edible shellfish on the Sound, in his opinion.

Then he saw something that made his eyes sparkle with excitement: a neck much like a horse clam, except that it had two openings instead of one, and it spouted a *double* fountain. A goeduck!

Bart stood stock still, trying to mark the spot with his eyes. That big, barnacle-covered rock for one landmark,

and that group of five starfish, intertwined, for another—
and about so far from the tenth piling. Yes, he thought he
could find it again. He turned quietly and hurried back to
camp.

"Wake up, guys!" Bart shook first one boy, then another,
and then the third. "Get up! It's a minus tide and there are
goeducks here."

It took him a minute to rouse them, but when he repeated
the magic word "goeduck" Vic and Parker rolled out and
grabbed their shoes.

Steve opened his eyes reluctantly. With his ashstreaked
face, he looked like a sleepy clown. "What's all the excitement about? What's a gooey duck, or whatever it is?"

"Didn't you ever hear of a goeduck?" Bart asked incredulously. "Why, it's the finest shellfish in this part of the country." While Vic and Parker laced their shoes and pulled on
their jackets, Bart threw more wood on the fire. Then he
caught up the cooking pot and searched among the shells
that lined the shore for the largest horse clam shell he could
find. As he worked, he explained to Steve.

"It's a huge clam, really, or something like it. But it has a
different flavor. And it makes keen fritters and chowder and
even steaks. When Mother cooks them, Dad says it's a dish
fit for a king."

"They're getting pretty rare around here now, though,"
Vic observed, standing up.

"And it's real sport, digging them," Parker added.

Belatedly, Steve caught the excitement and rolled out of
bed. But the others did not wait for him. No one even
commented on his black face. They were off down the

79

beach before he had one shoe on.

Vic and Bart, while they could not claim to be experts at the sport of goeduck digging, had helped a couple of times to dig for them. Parker had never done anything but watch, and Steve knew nothing whatever about the sport.

And it was really sport! Speed and endurance were both essential, as well as strategy, for a goeduck could go down through the sand faster than a fellow could dig.

When he had located the ugly neck sticking up through the sand, Bart said, "We'll start digging off here to the side, and then when we think we're deep enough, we'll dig over to him."

With his big clam shell, Bart began to dig a couple of feet to the right of the ugly neck. Almost at once the neck disappeared.

"We'll have to hurry," said Vic. Dropping to his knees, facing Bart, he began to dig, too, alternating his strokes with Bart's, so that in a very short time they had a deep round hole.

"Do you think we're deep enough?" Bart asked, beginning to pant from his exertions.

"Let's go a little deeper to be sure," said Vic. "Better to be deeper than you need to be, rather than short of it." On they went, increasing the tempo of their scooping shells. Suddenly, as if at a signal, both boys threw down their shells and began to scoop with their hands.

"Now!" said Vic, and stopped digging.

Bart lay flat on the sand and lowered his head and shoulders into the hole. Down at the bottom, at the left of the excavation, he began to scoop out the sand in a lateral tunnel. Faster and faster he worked. The tunnel caved in and became a half-filled ditch. Still Bart worked on.

"Your turn now, Vic," he gasped at last, raising his shoulders from the hole and rolling out of the way. Instantly Vic took his place and continued the work on the ditch. Soon he made a lunge. When he withdrew his arm, he held a huge sand-covered shellfish.

"Got him!"

Bart clapped Vic on the back enthusiastically. "He's a beauty!"

Steve's face indicated that he saw nothing beautiful in the creature with the enormous brown neck. His tone revealed his lack of enthusiasm as he said, "Looks like he outgrew his shell."

Vic dropped the goeduck into the kettle Bart held out, and brushed the sand from his hands. "Goeducks don't look like much, but wait till you taste them. And boy! Is it sport to catch them! You wouldn't believe how fast those things can move through the sand."

Bart filled the kettle with sea water to cover the goeduck, and set it up on the beach. "If there's one goeduck here, there ought to be others," he reasoned, and the boys scattered to look for more.

Soon Parker called, "Here's one!"

Vic, who was nearest to him, ran to help. Bart went on past them, still searching the beach. No use stopping to help Parker and Vic. It was really a two-man job, digging for goeducks. A third could only stand and watch.

Suddenly Steve said, "Isn't that one?" He pointed to a big brown neck protruding from the sand and spurting a

81

single stream of water.

Bart started to say that it had only one opening, and therefore was a horse clam, when an idea struck him. A wonderful idea for a joke on Steve—ignorant, gullible Steve, who had never heard of a horse clam, probably.

"Why, it sure is! You spotted it, Steve, so it will be all yours." Bart dropped to his knees. "Come on, get to digging." He indicated a spot well to the side of the clam's neck, and Steve set to work with a will.

"You can't dig goeducks from the top," Bart went on, "for they can go down faster than you can dig. So you dig off to the side until you can come up under them."

It was all Bart could do to keep from laughing as he watched Steve digging earnestly away with all his might. He wanted to call the other boys to share in the joke, but they were still busy with their goeduck, and anyway, to tell the joke might be to spoil it.

Bart spelled Steve briefly, when the big boy began to pant hard, but Steve was so anxious to get his own goeduck that he insisted on taking over again very soon, and Bart gladly relinquished his place.

Vic and Parker came up just as Steve made a lunge at the end of his lateral ditch and grabbed for his "goeduck." He drew his hand out, puzzled. "There was nothing there."

"Quick!" cried Bart, pretending a need to hurry. "I'll dig down while you dig up. We'll find him."

As Bart had known he would, Steve found the shellfish very near the surface, where he had been all the time. Steve's deep hole had been totally unnecessary to get a slow-moving horse clam.

When Steve's fingers closed on the big clam, he drew it out proudly.

Vic's mouth dropped open. "Why, that's not a . . ."

Winking at his pal, Bart interrupted swiftly. "That's not a very *big* goeduck, Steve, but sometimes the smallest ones are the best eating."

Steve surveyed his catch proudly and went to put it in the kettle.

Parker smiled in appreciation of the joke, but Vic merely shrugged and turned away. He didn't approve of practical jokes, Bart knew, but he would not give this one away. And it was going to be such fun to hear Steve brag about his "goeduck." Wouldn't he feel cheap when he found out it was nothing but a worthless horse clam? Bart chuckled in anticipation and started to look for other goeducks—genuine ones this time.

9. THE FIGHT

TWO OTHER GOEDUCKS GOT AWAY, BUT the boys finally managed to capture one more.

"Perfect!" exclaimed Bart. "Now we've each got one to take home."

"Aren't we going to cook them here?" asked Steve.

"Too much work to clean them," Vic explained. "Besides, you need a long, sharp knife. They'll keep all right till we get home. It isn't so warm today."

"Let's get breakfast," Parker urged. "I'm starved."

It was Steve's turn to provide the meal. Bart watched curiously to see if Steve knew anything at all about camp cooking—or any other kind of cooking, for that matter.

He soon decided that Steve had never been around food before, except to eat it. He didn't know enough to dilute the canned milk with water for cocoa until Vic told him. He hadn't the slightest idea how to fry the bacon until Parker showed him. But he did manage to get the oranges out of the sack and give one to each boy to be eating while he (Steve) cooked the bacon and eggs.

Squeezing their oranges greedily, Vic and Bart and Parker sauntered over to the boat while they waited for breakfast. They removed the canvas covering and stowed it away up forward, figuring aloud how long it would be before the tide would be in.

As they turned back toward the fire, Bart gasped. "Look at that dumb cluck! He's going to set himself afire if he doesn't watch out!"

"He sure is," agreed Vic, starting to run.

Steve had discarded, for some unknown reason, the long stick which Parker had thrust through the rings in the frying pan handle to provide a heat-proof grip at a bearable distance from the campfire. Now the short handle was obviously growing too hot for him and he did not know what to do, having nothing to rest the pan on. Juggling the frying pan from one hand to the other, he tipped it. Out poured bacon fat onto the fire, and the flames blazed high in an instant. They licked at Steve's hand and caught his jacket sleeve.

Almost before Steve's scream could split the air, Vic was upon him, with Bart and Parker only a step behind. Vic pushed against Steve with all his might, shoving him away from the fire and down on the beach. Quick as a flash he scooped sand over the burning sleeve.

In a few seconds the fire was out, but Steve's hand was burned quite painfully.

"Where's the first aid kit?" asked Vic.

They all looked blankly at each other. No one said anything.

85

"Well, *somebody* was supposed to bring it," Vic insisted. "We divided up everything we thought we'd need, and each one took the responsibility for the food for one meal, and for one other thing. I had the food for lunch today, and the canteen."

Bart said, "I had last night's dinner, and the cook kit."

Parker said, "I had the boat and the gas, and the axe. You fellows said I didn't need to bring any food."

"That's right." Vic and Bart nodded.

Steve smiled sheepishly in spite of the pain from his hand. "Guess I'm the guilty one," he admitted. "Al told me to bring a first aid kit, but I didn't have any, and . . ."

He did not finish, but they knew what he meant. He had no more money and he didn't like to borrow. If he had not been a tenderfoot, he would have known that a first aid kit is one thing you must have when you go on a trip, no matter where you have to borrow it.

Vic frowned. "We ought to get something on that hand. There isn't even anything clean for bandages, is there?"

Suddenly Bart had an idea. He darted to his packsack and fished around in its depths. "I've got it!" he cried triumphantly, bringing out a couple of tea bags left over from last night's dinner.

"What's the idea of tea when we have cocoa?" asked Steve stupidly. "I didn't spill the cocoa, did I?"

Bart poured some water into a tin cup and set it at the edge of the fire to heat. "The tea is for your hand," he explained. "Nothing better for a burn than tannic acid, and tea is full of that. We'll soak the tea bags in hot water and

86

then bind them over your burn. That'll hold it till we get home."

The bacon was a total loss, of course, having dropped in the fire when Steve tipped the pan. But Vic scrambled the eggs and Parker buttered the bread and poured the cocoa. By the time Bart had Steve's hand bandaged, using his hand-kerchief to tie the tea bags over the burn, breakfast was ready.

As he finished the last bite of scrambled eggs, Parker re-marked, "It seems a lot later than eight-thirty, doesn't it?"

It certainly did. Bart had thought it was mid-morning, at least, so much had happened since he woke up in the cold gray dawn.

"We'll leave right after lunch," Parker went on. "I prom-ised Dad I'd have the boat back early."

"Well, what are we waiting for?" cried Bart. "Let's have fun while we can. Anybody for more exploring?"

Parker joined him instantly. "I want to examine that sandstone ledge on the east side of the island. There might be some fossil clams there, and the museum is awfully anx-ious to get some."

As Bart and Parker started off, they heard Vic say, "I'll do your clean-up for you, Steve. That hand must hurt pretty bad."

Bart flushed in shame that he had not thought to offer to help, but he did not turn back.

Bart knew little about geology. He doubted that Parker knew much more, but the latter put on a good show, at least. He talked glibly of glacial age, volcanic rock, earth faults,

87

and so on. Bart scarcely listened as he clambered over the ledge and stopped now and then to dig out an intriguing bit with his knife.

"All this island was under the sea a couple of million years ago," Parker proclaimed. "In fact, most of the West . . ."

For several minutes Bart had been noticing odd markings in the sandstone at his feet: small white arcs and semi-circles here and there, forming an interesting pattern. He stooped to investigate. Why, those white lines looked like the edges of shells! Could they be fossil clams?

Using his knife for a chisel and a stone for a hammer, Bart pried some of them out of the sandstone. Sure enough, they looked like stone clamshells, broken off.

He looked around for Parker, but he had disappeared around the cliff. Bart started to call to him, but he closed his mouth again and went on examining the ledge. This was *his* find. No use letting Parker in on it.

Then Bart saw a grooved white hump embedded in the sandstone. It looked like a perfect clam. He pried loose the hunk of sandstone that held the shell. He wouldn't try to get the thing out for fear of breaking it.

As Bart knelt there, examining his find, Parker came back. "I haven't found a thing," he said gloomily.

Bart smiled in satisfaction. "I have. Look at this, Park."

Parker whistled. "A fossil clam! Just what I wanted."

He attempted to take it from Bart's hand, but Bart drew it back. "No, you don't. I found it, and it's mine."

"But the museum . . ."

"The museum will be just as glad to get it from me as from you," Bart answered cockily.

A pebble rolled down the slope and he looked up. There stood Vic and Steve. Vic looked very high-and-mighty, the way he looked when you did something he did not approve of.

Holding onto the fossil clam, Bart moved away, pretending not to have seen the new arrivals. He tried to tell himself he didn't care what Vic thought. He had found the fossil clam and he had a perfect right to keep it. Parker was just being unreasonable in expecting him to give it up. All right, so he never would have thought of looking for it if Park had not suggested it, but that didn't change anything. He would *not* give it up. It would be a real thrill to go to the museum and give it to them. They would put it on display with a sign which would read, "Donated by Barton Skinner, found on Ecklund's Island."

Let Parker find a fossil himself. Since there was one perfect fossil, there might be others.

Bart spent the rest of the morning exploring alone.

But when he returned to camp at noon, Parker had not succeeded in finding anything but fragments of fossil clams, and he was still sore. So was Vic. But Bart pretended not to notice. He acted as if everything were perfectly okay. He chattered and joked and ignored the fact that Steve was the only one who responded.

By noon the tide was in, and the three boys went in swimming again. This time Steve's burned hand made a fine excuse for him to stay out of the water.

"I'll bet he wouldn't have gone in, anyway," Bart said to himself disgustedly. "He's chicken." But he had an uneasy feeling that his own fool stunt at Lexy's beach party (pulling Steve's legs out from under him) had intensified the big fellow's fear of the water and his reluctance to learn to swim.

The water was fairly warm, for the Sound. The tide had come in over sun-warmed sand. Since Vic and Parker still showed no disposition to be friendly, Bart swam way out in the deep water. He turned over on his back and, with his hands behind his head, he floated off alone.

He should have been perfectly happy. He dearly loved to swim, especially away from the town like this, with invigorating salt water under him, sunshine above him, and the blue sky dotted with feathery clouds. If only the other fellows liked him! He had always thought Vic was his friend, but on this trip . . . Was Steve trying to take Vic away from him as he was obviously attempting to do with Lexy? At the thought Bart turned over and swam vigorously toward shore. He would see about that!

But Vic did not give him a chance to do anything about it. He remained aloof, getting out of the water at Bart's approach and starting the fire for lunch.

After Vic's lunch of peanut butter sandwiches and canned soup, they all worked together to push the boat into the water. Then, while Vic cleaned up the few dishes, the others loaded the sleeping bags and the kettle of goeducks in the boat.

"Not a scrap of food left to go back," Bart observed. "What if we're marooned somewhere and can't get home?"

Steve grinned. "Couldn't we cook our goeducks?"

"Sure. Each one can eat his own." As he went to see that the fire was completely out, Bart chuckled at the image of Steve struggling to chew his tough horse clam.

"Ready?" called Parker. "Then all aboard. Let's shove off. The wind is coming up. We may get rough weather."

Bart watched Ecklund's Island grow smaller and smaller in the distance. He had had a good time, in spots. But somehow, the week-end left quite a bit to be desired. There had not been nearly as much excitement as he had hoped for.

Certainly this trip back was dull, with everybody quiet, nobody talking at all. He'd better liven it up a bit.

"Bet I can beat anybody walking on my hands around the deck."

"You mean *now?*" asked Parker doubtfully. "While we're moving at twelve knots?"

"Sure! Nothing to it. Watch this." Bart stripped down to his underwear and climbed up on the foredeck.

"Don't be stupid, Bart." Vic's voice, usually gentle, was sharp. "That could be dangerous. And what good would it do?"

Bart paid no attention. He was crawling out on the deck. The slope of the smooth deck was gentle enough, but the boat, bucking a freshing wind, slapped each wave with a thud. Bart saw that his stunt would be more difficult than he had bargained for, but he would not back down now.

He raised up on his hands at last and balanced, getting the rhythm of the slapping waves. It was sort of like riding a bucking broncho. There. Now he had the rhythm. He began to walk on his hands, a careful step at a time. One, two, three . . . He had reached the prow. Now to turn and go back down the port side.

Just as Bart was balancing after the turn, the boat hit another wave. The thud was harder than usual. It threw Bart off balance. When he felt himself falling, he turned so as to make a clean dive, clear of the cruiser and the dangerous propeller.

He came up, sputtering, fifty feet from the boat. Parker put the craft about and cut the motor, drifting up beside him. Bart climbed over the side, dripping and shivering but laughing.

"See," he said to Vic, "it wasn't dangerous at all."

Vic just looked at him without answering, and Bart stripped off his sopping underwear and pulled on a dry shirt and slacks.

As the trip drew to a close, Bart tried to account for his feeling of depression. He came to the conclusion that it was because of Steve and his dumbness and clumsiness. Steve always spoiled everything for him.

He said as much to Vic as the two of them walked home from Parker's, after thanking their host, and expressing their appreciation to his father and mother.

"Steve spoils everything," Bart concluded.

Vic looked down at him with his high-and-mighty expression. What was wrong with him now?

This time Vic let Bart know exactly what was wrong.

"You make me tired, Bart Skinner." Vic began in his usual gentle drawl, but his voice rose higher and faster as he proceeded. "You're always showing off, always trying to make somebody else uncomfortable. And you keep blaming other people for your own mistakes."

"Why . . . why . . ." Bart fairly sputtered, he was so surprised and hurt. For Vic to turn against him!

"It wasn't Steve that spoiled that trip," Vic went on, really hot now. "If anybody spoiled it, it was you. You acted like a selfish brat. You and your stupid jokes, and your show-off stunts! Why don't you act your age?"

Bart dropped his sleeping bag and packsack and faced Vic there on the beach. His anger had risen with every word Vic had spoken and now he was boiling mad.

"You can't talk to me like that! Nobody can say things like that to me and get away with it." Bart drew back his fist and let Vic have it, right on the jaw. Vic staggered. He dropped his camping things. But he did not strike back.

Bart danced around him on his toes. "Why don't you hit me?" he taunted. "Why don't you hit me? Or are you too pure and noble to fight? You think you're better than anybody else, don't you? You . . . you . . ."

Vic flushed a brick red, but he made no move to hit back. "I couldn't hit a kid as small as you," he said loftily.

Nothing he could have said would have made Bart more furious.

"You'll hit me or else you'll run, because I'm going to murder you!" he yelled, wading into Vic with both fists. "Chicken! Too chicken to fight!" *Wham!* He connected with Vic's jaw again.

At last Vic sprang into action. He landed a haymaker in Bart's stomach that knocked his wind out. Bart folded up like a jackknife.

"You little brat!" *Sock!* "*Some*body ought to hit you!" *Wham!* "Knock some sense into you." *Bop!*

93

Bart tried to fight back, but it was no use. Vic was a flailing, punching hurricane. This was a Vic he had never seen—and one he hoped never to encounter again. Bart felt as if he were being punched on all sides. He had to fall down or run. If he fell down, he would have to face Vic, and he couldn't face him. He ducked Vic's last punch and ran.

10. THE NEW CHEER LEADER

WITH HIS USUAL COCKINESS, BART WALKED into the room where the cheer-leader finals were to be held.

The room filled quickly with spectators, Mr. Boone among them, of course. Vic, the chairman, rapped for order.

Bart had not seen Vic, except at a distance, since their fight on the beach. Now he looked curiously at his erstwhile friend, to see how their quarrel had affected him. Vic's jaw was slightly discolored, but that was the only sign Bart could see of their encounter. It was quite a blow to Bart to see that Vic's expression was serene and cheerful, as if it didn't bother him at all to lose a friend.

Okay! If that was the way Vic wanted it, Bart would never let on that he had any regrets, any more than he would let anyone know of the physical soreness Vic's blows had left on his body.

Bart shrugged Vic off his mind and looked around at his fellow contestants. There were only three this time: Steve, in the seat behind him, with a bandage on his burned hand,

95

and Al across the aisle.

Vic explained the procedure. Today the contestants could not choose their cheers. All of them had to try out on each yell the committee specified. They would begin with an easy cheer, "Yea, Team," and Bart would start.

After three of the trials Bart knew that Al had no chance. The decision lay between Steve, and Bart, himself. And each new yell they tried increased his certainty that the race would be close. Steve had obviously been practising intensively since the preliminary tryouts, whereas Bart had given little time to it.

While Steve exhibited his technique with "Hi, Hi, Harbor High," Bart slid down in the seat to rest. Fortunately, the contestants were not expected, today, to take part in yells they were not leading.

Bart ran his tongue around his dry mouth. He would like a drink of water, but he did not want to miss any of his rivals' performances. Gum might help that dryness; he took a package of bubble gum from his pocket and popped a piece into his mouth.

As he chewed thoughtfully and watched Steve's actions closely, Bart's determination to win the post of yell leader for Harbor High rose to fever pitch. He *had* to win. He had to show this school and this town that he could *do* something, *be* somebody, even if he was a "half-pint."

Steve sat down amid waves of applause. Vic announced the next yell. He nodded to Bart, and the boy rose to his feet. He took the gum from his mouth and parked it under the edge of his desk.

Summoning all of his genuine enthusiasm for the task,

96

Bart sprang lightly to the front of the room.

"Okay, gang! On your feet. Our team is trailing by two touchdowns, and they're getting discouraged. Let's show them we're behind them, we know they can win. Let's *make* them win!"

Smiling at this fanciful pretense that they were actually at a football game, the spectators rose at his bidding.

"Let's go!" Bart put every gyration and gesture he could think of into that yell. The others caught his enthusiasm and outdid themselves. The room rocked with sound. When Bart finished with a leap worthy of a professional tumbler, and flip-flopped to his seat, they clapped and cheered. All over the room Bart heard exclamations of approval. "Swell." "Neat." "Terrific." He sat down, breathing hard from exertion and glowing with satisfaction. Let Steve beat that performance, if he could!

Bart's mouth felt dryer than ever. He dislodged his gum from its parking place and stuck it in his mouth.

As usual, Al's performance was adequate but uninspired. Popping his gum absently, Bart watched and listened. No competition there. Al would never get the vote. But Steve . . . that was a different matter. Steve lacked Bart's lightness and agility, but for some reason his shy smile seemed as much of a spur to the volunteer cheering section as Bart's exuberance. If Steve did as well with this "Yackety-Yak" as he had with the others, he might be the committee's choice!

Bart chewed harder than ever. This was the first time he had allowed himself to face the possibility that he might lose out in the contest for cheer leader. Why did Steve have to try out for this job? Surely there were plenty of other things he could do. He was heavy enough for football, tall enough for basketball. It wasn't fair that he should horn in on this yell leader business—the only job that Bart could handle.

Suddenly Bart's resentment, which had smoldered so long unseen, burst into flame, just as the beach fire had smoldered for hours before leaping into life—his resentment against Steve for his effortless popularity, for his success with Lexy, for causing trouble between him and Vic, for his dumbness in fishing and swimming and putting out beach fires, for his clumsiness and uncontrolled strength in breaking records and oars (although Steve had brought him a new oar only the night before). He had to do something to keep Steve from winning this contest. Some way, somehow, he had to slow him down. But how? That was the question. What *could* he do?

In an effort to concentrate on the problem, Bart stopped chewing. Frantically he cast about in his mind for a solution. His tongue rolled the gum around in his mouth. Absently he looked down at Steve's big feet, stuck out in the aisle beside him.

Suddenly, Bart drew the gum from his mouth. Quick as a flash, he plastered the wad of gum in the center of Steve's shoe sole.

Al finished and sat down. The chairman nodded to Steve. Slowly the big fellow withdrew his long legs from the aisle and rose. He started to step away from his desk. Then he stopped and looked down at his feet, a puzzled look on his face.

Again Steve started down the aisle. This time he kept going, but his right foot clung to the wood at every step, pulling long strands of gum with it, which slowed his progress, and embarrassed him.

When he reached the front of the room Steve paused and looked at Vic. "Would you mind . . . would it be all right if I take off my shoes? I must have stepped in something."

He stooped, loosened the laces of both shoes, and slipped them off. Standing in his stockings, he straightened to his full six feet and grinned at the rest of the room.

"Ready?" he raised his long arms. The group rose and stood, attentive, waiting for his signal. "Okay."

"Yackety, yackety, yackety yak! Clackety clack! Clackety clack! Yackety, yackety, yackety yak . . ."

Bart's face burned with disappointment and shame as he watched and listened. What a stupid trick! What had got into him? And it hadn't worked, after all. Steve had pulled a trick of his own, just taking off the annoying shoes.

"Clackety clack, clackety clack . . ."

Well, he was thankful for one thing, Bart thought glumly: no one had seen him put that gum on Steve's shoe, he was sure. Everyone had been watching Al.

The yell ended. The fellows cheered and whistled as Steve retrieved his shoes and returned to his seat. The chairman made a mark on his paper and looked up.

"That's all, fellows," Vic announced. "The committee will meet right away to make its decision. We'll post it on the bulletin board."

Bart followed the others into the hall. He ought to go on

over to the fountain and get to work; Mr. Willoughby
wouldn't like his being late again. But he wanted to know
the committee's decision, and he didn't want to wait until
morning.

Bart found himself the center of a gang of congratulatory
boys, who took it for granted he was going directly to the
Malt Shop. He could not avoid accompanying them without
making some excuse, and he couldn't think of a good one.

Anyway, their praises sounded sweet in Bart's ears. They
seemed certain that he would win. They began to ask his
advice, as if he were already the official Harbor High yell
leader.

"Don't you think we ought to get some new yells, Bart?"

"I heard a good one last week at the View Crest game.
See what you think of this . . ."

"The cheering section is pretty important to the team,
isn't it, Bart?"

"Do you think the girls ought to have a cheer leader, too,
or . . ."

They had reached the Malt Shop and still Bart had not
thought of an excuse to get away from them. If he went in
to work, he might not find out the decision of the committee before morning, for the school would be locked by
the time he was finished. Suddenly he had an idea . . . why
hadn't he thought of it before?

"Rats! I forgot my history. Got to go and get it."

He waved to the other fellows and dashed back toward
the school.

Vic and Mr. Boone stood side by side in front of the
bulletin board as Bart raced in, out of breath. The Freshman

Class president pushed another thumbtack through the notice he held and turned away, evading his friend's eyes. But the principal made no attempt to avoid Bart. He stood, waiting, while the boy approached.

"You wanted to learn the decision of the committee, Barton?"

"Yes, sir. I was . . . interested."

"Help yourself."

Bart looked up at the notice. Scrawled in black pencil, untidy but unmistakable, were the words: "Yell leader, Steve Huber."

In spite of himself, Bart gasped. The principal looked down at him.

"Surprised?"

"Well, he's good, of course." Bart squirmed, regretting his decision to come back. Why couldn't old Boone-goon let him alone? Wasn't it bad enough to lose—and to his rival—without being needled about it?

"Would you like to know why he won?"

"Why, because the committee thought he was best, I suppose."

"No, the committee thought *you* were best."

"Then why . . ."

Mr. Boone's voice grew biting sharp. "Do you need to ask?"

Bart dropped his eyes before the scorn in the principal's gaze.

"We have standards at this school, Barton—standards of honesty, of fair play, of sportsmanship. When a boy tries to win by playing dirty tricks on a fellow contestant, we

101

consider that he has disqualified himself."

Bart could not find a word to say. So someone had seen him. Someone had told!

"I've been watching you ever since you came to Harbor High, Barton," Mr. Boone went on. His voice was not as sharp now, but Bart longed desperately for it to stop so he could escape. "You have a lot of ability. You are one of the most capable students we have had. But you spoil everything you do by wondering if other people are watching and admiring. You're always playing to the gallery, always showing off, always acting the clown. You'll do anything to get attention, to get your own way, to win out over someone else."

Mr. Boone paused, and Bart turned away. "Wait. I'm not through yet." Bart stirred restively. "Why don't you 'get wise to yourself' as the boys say? Why don't you learn that the important thing is not *whether* you win, but *how* you win . . . or lose."

Bart finally managed to break away. He hurried past the Malt Shop and went straight on home, quickening his steps increasingly until he was running at top speed. He could not bear to work at the fountain today. He could not hide from other people his dreadful knowledge that he had lost the cheer leader job to Steve. He simply could not face anyone today.

11. LOST IN THE FOG

BART HAD NEARLY REACHED HIS OWN GATE when he realized that he couldn't face his own family any more than he could have endured the fellows at the Malt Shop. He couldn't answer "Okay" to his mother's daily question about school, and he knew just how piercingly she would look at him if he evaded answering. He used to tell her about his little troubles at school, Bart remembered, but ever since he had begun to realize that he was doomed to be a runt, he had clammed up. This problem was too big and too important to confide in anyone.

Bart slipped around to the basement door. He would go out in the boat. He would fish until dinnertime. Perhaps by then he would have regained sufficient self-control to hide his feelings from the rest of the family.

If only he didn't run into Eddie now! Thank goodness, the basement was empty! Eddie must not be through with his paper route. Bart grabbed oars, net, fishing rod and tackle box and sneaked down to the beach. He wouldn't bother with the motor, for that would mean another trip into the house. Better to slip away before he ran into anyone—row out on the water where he could be alone, where he could get hold of himself.

The beach, still desolate looking with its charred reminders of the fire, was deserted. Good—no one to ask questions! Bart pushed the boat over the sand and into the water. Quickly he tossed in his gear, shoved the skiff out, and jumped aboard. Fitting the oars into the oarlocks, he pulled away from the shore. The sun had gone behind a cloud. No matter. What good was sunshine when you felt black as night inside?

For a few minutes Bart put all of his strength into rowing. Get out of sight of the house, away from shore, where nobody could pester, where nobody could call him back.

Alone at last, way out in the bay, Bart shipped his oars and opened his tackle box. He would not try to troll. Mooching was easier when you were alone. Automatically, his fingers went through the motions of rigging his rod and stringing his line. No bait today; no matter. Use a spoon. His mind took no notice of what his fingers did. His thoughts were a veritable tornado of stinging memories that chased themselves around in ever-increasing fury.

"Yell leader, Steve Huber." "We have standards of fair play." "You'll do anything to get attention." "Yell leader, Steve Huber." "I don't like to be conspicuous." "Get wise to yourself." "Yell leader, Steve Huber." "Poor sport." "Yell leader, Steve Huber." "I want to go with Steve." Steve . . . Steve . . . Steve . . .

His line out, Bart began to row. A few strokes, then rest

on the oars. Then a few more strokes, and rest again. He looked at his pole with un-seeing eyes, while his thoughts spun faster and faster, closing in around the one word— Steve. Bart's resentment against Lexy and Mr. Boone, his soreness at Vic, his humiliation at losing the cheer leader job—everything revolved around Steve. Somehow Steve was responsible for everything that had happened and everything that seemed likely to happen. The desire to beat Steve became an obsession. He *had* to beat him in *something!*

A tug on his line told Bart he had a strike. But the knowledge did not bring the usual thrill, the anticipation of a good fight. He felt too sore, too hurt and humiliated, to be excited by the prospect of catching a fish. His chest still ached—from running home so fast, Bart tried to tell himself, knowing full well that kind of an ache would have disappeared long ago. His throat hurt where a big lump refused to be swallowed.

The reel zinged. Far off to the side of the boat, a fish jumped—a silver salmon, a fair-sized one, too. Bart had him hooked, all right. He began to play his fish.

Let him take all the line he wants. Then reel in. More line. Then bring him in. Bart's fingers worked by themselves; his mind remained aloof from mere sport and continued to whirl around its focal point of "Steve." How could he get revenge? How could he take Steve down a peg? How could he pay him off for taking friends and honors which Bart felt should be his?

The salmon allowed himself to be brought in close to the boat. Then he took off like a streak of lightning; line ran out again. Bart's mind paid little heed, but his trained fingers proved equal to their task. He played his fish expertly, automatically, and netted him safely, all with scarcely a trace of the exhilaration and satisfaction which usually accompanied a catch. He put his line out again and continued to fish. Row a little, then rest on the oars . . . a few more strokes . . .

Bart's thoughts began to slow down in their frantic whirl. His mind tried to follow a straight line, to plan some way to make his dream of triumph over Steve come true. But instead of following a straight and practical path, his thoughts veered off on tangents, picturing one daydream after another, of victories over Steve. . . .

Bart is pursuing his own course down the school corridor, calm and dignified, when Mr. Boone comes up to him. In front of dozens of students, the principal drops to his knees and begs Bart to take over as yell leader. The cheering section has fallen down on its job of keeping up enthusiasm for the team, he says; Steve is unequal to this important task. Everyone wants Bart. The students crowd around and entreat him to be their yell king. Magnanimously Bart agrees to help them out. . . .

Row a bit, then rest. . . . Row, and rest. . . .

Now Bart is riding his rattle-trap bicycle down the hill from school. Ahead of him Steve, also on his bike, hits a small child and thrusts her into the path of a speeding car. Quick as thought, Bart hurls himself from his bike. He snatches the child and throws her clear, but is hit, himself, by the car's fender. Surrounded by a crowd of admiring and grateful bystanders, Bart points to the penitent Steve who hovers near, and says to the policeman, "Arrest that boy!"

Another strike. Play the fish.

Now Bart is putting his brains to work on a mystery that has baffled teachers and students at Harbor High for weeks. Things have been disappearing out of lockers, and the principal is at his wits' end to find the culprit. Bart, working astutely and quietly, finds clue after clue. He stations himself out of sight in the locker room and catches Steve in the act of rifling a classmate's locker. Mr. Boone shakes Bart's hand gratefully and introduces him to the student body at an assembly as a benefactor of Harbor High—one of the keenest minds the principal has ever met.

While Bart's mind pictured these pleasing scenes of honor for himself and degradation for Steve, his hands kept on with their fishing. He netted the second fish, then a third. None of them was large—not over two pounds. But they were nice salmon. They would be good eating.

It was when he felt his fourth strike that Bart suddenly woke to the change in the weather. He sensed the tug on the line which meant a bite. He heard the splash which indicated that the salmon had jumped out of the water. But he could scarcely see the fish.

Daydreams and thoughts of revenge vanished in a flash. Bart's mind came down to reality with a thud. Fog had crept in silently, insidiously. He could not see fifty yards away from his boat!

For a few seconds Bart stared unbelievingly about him. Surely the fog could not have closed in without his noticing it! When he left home the weather, while overcast, had been clear enough to see the opposite shore of the bay. Now he could not even see the shore on this side, much

107

less the far side of the harbor.

Moving fast, Bart reeled in his line, so quickly that the leader broke. But he wasted no time regretting the lost fish. He took hold of the oars and began to row.

All of a sudden a horrible thought froze his hands on the oars: how did he know he was heading for home? How did he know that Harbor City lay in this direction, an easy pull on the oars? It *seemed* as if he were headed south, but how did he *know?* His boat might have swung completely around while he was mooching, for he had paid no attention to directions. He might be headed north instead of south. The tide was going out; it might have carried him completely out of the harbor and into the middle of Puget Sound. How could he tell, when he could see nothing in any direction, except an occasional seagull or a piece of driftwood?

Bart rested on his oars. Worse than useless to row until he knew in which direction to go. He peered around him, trying to pierce the curtain of gray fog, trying to find some clue as to his location. No use. The whole world was a damp, formless, colorless cloud, with Bart and his skiff in the center of it.

Might as well face it: he was in a serious predicament. There was little hope that another fisherman, who had kept his eyes open and knew in which direction he was heading, would pass near enough to hail. Any fisherman with a grain of sense would have pulled for shore when he saw the fog closing in. Anyway, Bart had not seen any other fisher-men: not that that meant anything, he admitted ruefully to himself. He had been so absorbed in bitter thoughts and

daydreams that there could have been a dozen boats out in the bay and he would not have noticed them.

He could not hope that the fog would rise again as quickly and as silently as it had fallen. Here in the North-west, on Puget Sound, September often brought fogs which lasted for hours, even days.

The water remained smooth—no wind. But the air grew colder by the minute. Bart shivered. His red zipper jacket gave slight protection against this penetrating dampness;

he had not thought to bring a parka. If he had to sit out here all night: Bart shuddered at the thought. Could night be far off? He had no idea of the time—no watch. There had been no sunset. How long had he been fishing? He did not know. He did not even know what time he had started.

Mom would not miss him until she served dinner. Then she would be cross because he was late. After a while she would become worried, and Dad—if he were home yet— would get very stern. Perhaps he would even set out to look for his son—only nobody knew where he was. Even if Dad found the boat missing and guessed Bart had gone fishing, how could anyone find him in this fog?

A faint sound caught the boy's ear, a low, steady, throbbing noise. Now a whistle tooted far off. A boat! A big one, either a freighter or a ferry. Bart leaned forward eagerly. Help at last! He shouted at the top of his voice. "Help! Help!"

The engine's sound grew louder. The ghostly whistle came closer. Still Bart could not see the ship.

He screamed at the top of his lungs, "Help! Help!"

The thud of the ship's engines became a menacing roar. Its fog whistle seemed to blast right in Bart's ears. And still he could see nothing.

Then, suddenly, there it was, right on top of him, a giant black hulk whose steep side seemed to tower up to the sky which he could not see!

All at once pure horror gripped Bart. The ship was going to run him down! They had not seen him at all, since he had no light to pierce the fog and warn them—not even a flashlight. They had not heard his cries over the clamor

110

of their own engines and the blast of their own fog whistle. In place of promising assistance, the ship was a horrible menace. Unless he could get out of the way fast, it was going to run him down! His hands tightened instinctively on the oars.

Terror stuck Bart's tongue to the roof of his mouth, but it lent iron to the muscles of his arms. He pulled on the oars as he had never pulled before. Quick, strong strokes, as if he were rowing in a varsity crew race. Pull, pull, pull. Row for dear life—and that was exactly what he was doing.

There! He had done it! The towering black hulk was sliding past the stern of his boat, a great, horrible, threatening wall of steel. It had missed his skiff by no more than a yard or two.

As full realization of the narrowness of his escape penetrated his consciousness, Bart crumpled up in the boat, his heart pounding, his muscles like jelly.

Instantly, however, he was threatened by another crisis. The ship's swells were upon him. There was no time to turn the boat to take them on the bow, and there was great danger of swamping. All he could do was hold the oars as steady as possible and ride the swells out.

His boat rocked and pitched. Wow! He shipped water that time. Bart gritted his teeth and held on. If he could just hold out for a few more seconds, the force of the swells would begin to diminish.

The ship's whistle was much fainter now as it disappeared in the fog. The thud of the engine faded out. By the time the swells had definitely ceased, Bart could no longer hear any sound of the vessel.

If only he knew where the ship was going, he might be able to calculate his own position. Was it going to Seattle? Or Tacoma? Or across the Sound to Bremerton, to the Navy Yard? Or was it headed toward the Straits of Juan de Fuca and the Pacific Ocean? There was no way of knowing.

The sea was smooth again. Once more the tiny row-boat drifted in a soundless, formless cloud. Bart fought down a rising panic. Wasn't there something he could do besides just sit here? Was he to sit here in the drifting boat and freeze—and starve? Or be run down by another boat that he could not get away from in time?

Maybe it would be better to row, even if he did not know where he was going. He would at least be warmer then. But he might tire himself out and be unable to row when he needed to.

Why, oh why, had he let himself get into this fix? Why hadn't he kept his wits about him and his mind on what he was doing, instead of losing himself in daydreams? Then he would have noticed the change in weather in time to get ashore before the beach became blotted out in fog.

And his daydreams had been useless and silly; he knew that, now. He had been at fault in the cheer leader business. He had deserved Mr. Boone's scolding and Vic's bawling out. He hadn't played fair. And he was a show-off and a poor loser and a poor sport. He was a drip and he hated himself.

But if he ever got out of this predicament, he would do better, Bart vowed. He would try—he really would—to

112

be a good sport. He would congratulate Steve on his victory in the cheer leader contest, and he would never let anyone suspect how he hated to lose. And he would make friends with Vic again. . . .

The fog was thicker than ever now, cold and gray and menacing, a smothering blanket about him. No sound broke the silence except the whisper of the dying swells against the boat.

He remembered another time when he had been caught out on the bay in a fog. But that time he had not been alone; Dad had been in the skiff with him. It was during the Kids' Fishing Derby, the first year that Bart, ten years old then, had been eligible for it. When the Derby was half over, fog had gathered rapidly until it became difficult to see even the nearest of the hundred boats in the bay.

There had been no danger then, however. Over the loudspeaker from Derby Headquarters at Harbor Park, officials had blared warnings to all boats to come in to shore, to come in carefully at low speed. Coast Guard boats, patrolling the boundaries of the Derby, had called the same warning. And the fog horn at the lighthouse had blasted monotonous and insistent appeals for caution.

Bart's heart gave a sudden leap. The fog horn! He would get home tonight, after all! The lighthouse fog horn would start at any minute, and all he would have to do would be to row toward the sound, then follow the beach two blocks east and he would be home!

The boy laughed aloud in sheer relief. It was just a matter of waiting and listening now. Odd that the fog horn had not started up long before this. But Bart knew that often it blew when Harbor City residents could see no reason for its warning, and sometimes it remained quiet when fog enveloped the city. Visibility on the ship channels did not always parallel visibility on shore. But with a fog like this over the water, the fog horn could be depended on to sound its warning soon.

Or had he drifted too far from the harbor to hear it? Bart dismissed that worry as soon as it appeared. That fog horn was audible for many miles. He would hear it all right; no doubt about that.

He settled himself to wait and listen. He pulled the collar of his jacket closer around his neck, and fumbled in his pockets in the vain hope of finding a forgotten candy bar that would take the edge off his ravenous appetite. But he found only a piece of bubble gum. The sight of it reminded him of his childish trick on Steve, the trick that had boomeranged. With a gesture of disgust, he tossed the gum over the side of the boat.

What was that? Bart strained his ears through the gloom. There it came again: a deep, low, rumbling, far-away boom. A few seconds of silence, then the boom again. That was it! The fog horn had started. Bart reached for his oars, but he paused and listened again. He was not going to rush into action this time, without being sure where it would lead him; he would be certain that this was the Harbor Lighthouse fog horn before he made a move.

Boom! Instantly Bart began to count rhythmically. "One. Two. Three." *Boom!* He started over: "One. Two. Three. Four. Five." *Boom!*

No doubt about it now. That was the fog horn at the Harbor City Lighthouse. No other fog horn on Puget Sound had exactly that same timing. Bart bent quickly to his oars.

Only one thing bothered him. The fog horn's blast seemed to come from the wrong direction. Surely the lighthouse should lie in back of him, instead of ahead and to the left. It was all Bart could do to persuade himself that the fault lay in his own sense of direction and not the lighthouse. It was easy to get turned around in the fog. He must forget his own ideas of direction and follow the booms. He pulled hard on his right oar until the bow of the boat pointed toward the ghostly booms of the fog horn.

Dip, pull, feather your oars . . . dip, pull, feather your oars . . . Difficult to tell the exact direction of the horn, but if he got too far off course, the sound would grow fainter. Bart rowed smoothly and strongly.

As he rowed, his thoughts went back to the Fishing Derby again. Just two and a half weeks now until this year's Derby. One good thing about losing out as yell king: he could put in more time fishing in preparation for the Derby.

The fog horn was growing louder now. Bart's steady stroke carried the boat on through the dark water. The fog had lifted a little, too.

A dim outline of the shore appeared on his left. Bart rested on his oars while he tried to decide just where he was. Then a flashing light, diffused by the fog, crossed his path. The lighthouse! He was almost home. He turned the boat parallel to the beach and rowed east.

A few minutes later Bart grounded the skiff on his own beach. All the lights in the house were on, and the yard lights as well. Home! Bart thought he had never seen such a beautiful sight in his life.

12. ANOTHER HALF-PINT

TRUE TO THE DECISION HE HAD MADE
while lost in the fog, the very next day Bart congratulated
Steve—although he would rather have taken the beating
his father promised him if he ever went out alone in the
boat again without permission. Steve seemed pleased at his
words, but not surprised.

The rest of Bart's self-imposed program proved much
harder. It was easy enough to *say* you would no longer be
a show-off or a poor sport, but *doing* it was another matter.
Habits, Bart discovered, can be extremely difficult to break.
Each time he got up to recite in a class, he found the anticipatory grins of his classmates an irresistible invitation
to comic capers that would call forth laughs. Each time he
walked down the hall, or went to an assembly, or got on the
bus practically hidden in the midst of a gang of kids who
towered over him, the urge to do something spectacular to
make them notice him became overpowering. By sixth
period Bart realized miserably that he had not changed

117

at all; he was still the clown of Harbor High, the "Half-Pint" who was good for a laugh any time—but good for nothing else. And he had not made a single move to make up with Vic.

When he entered the Malt Shop after school, prepared to go to work, Mr. Willoughby greeted him coldly.

"Sorry, Bart, I've got another boy. You didn't show up yesterday."

Bart started to explain, but Mr. Willoughby interrupted him. "What's more, I'm fed up with your clowning at the fountain, so you're through. Here's the money I owe you." He handed Bart a few coins and turned to wait on a customer.

Bart walked home alone, his mood as black as yesterday's. Only today he did not dare go out fishing to calm himself down. Dad had given strict orders: Bart couldn't take the boat out for the rest of the week.

Mrs. Skinner looked up from her ironing in surprise as Bart stamped in through the door. "What's the matter, Son? Aren't you working today?"

Bart shook his head angrily. He looked at his mother. Although her hair was beginning to gray, she was as tiny and slim as a little girl—smaller than Lexy. Suddenly the fear that he would never grow any bigger than she became a horrible certainty. He glared at her and spoke venomously.

"Why did you have to be such a runt?"

Mrs. Skinner gasped. Her eyes opened wide, positively stricken.

Bart whammed his books onto a chair and stalked out through the door again. Gee! Now he had hurt her. *She*

couldn't help being small, any more than he could. Why
had he said that? Why did he always say and do the wrong
thing? Bart sat down on the front steps, feeling thoroughly
ashamed and very sorry for himself.

Eddie came down the street, delivering his papers. In the
vacant lot a gang of seventh graders were playing their
rough and tumble version of football. Eddie paused to watch.

"Can I play with you when I finish my papers?" His high,
childish voice came clearly to Bart's ears.

The boys untangled themselves from the heap of arms and
legs.

"Naw," the tallest one growled. "You're too little. We
don't want no runts on our team."

Eddie turned away. Rolling a paper, he came across the
street and threw it at Bart's feet. The older boy saw that his
brother was very close to tears. So Eddie, too, felt his
smallness keenly? He, too, had the same problem of competing with boys who were fast outstripping him in size.
Yet Eddie did not clown and show off as Bart, himself, did.
He was too shy and quiet.

Suddenly Bart knew that for that very reason Eddie suffered even more. On an impulse he asked, "Would you like
me to help you with the rest of your papers?"

Eddie's face lighted up with pleasure and surprise. "Sure!"

With four hands working instead of two, the paper
route was covered quickly. Several times Bart tried to say
something to comfort his brother for his rebuff from the
other boys, but he could not find the right words.

Not until the last paper had been delivered and the
brothers turned homeward did they have much to say to

119

each other. Then Eddie asked suddenly. "How come you're not working this afternoon?"

To his own surprise, Bart found himself telling his brother the whole story, about being fired, about losing out in the yell leader competition, about his fight with Vic— everything except Lexy's refusal to go with him to the Freshman Hop. Eddie listened quietly, with only an occasional exclamation of surprise or indignation.

When Bart finished, the younger boy merely said, "That's tough." But the sympathy in his voice was very comforting. Bart felt better than he had for hours.

"I've just *got* to win the Fishing Derby now," he declared.

Eddie sighed. "I'd like to win a prize, too. But I don't know how to fish like you do."

For the remainder of the walk home Eddie talked, shyly at first, then faster and more freely. He told Bart about his troubles and problems with his paper route and his school work and his playmates. He told of his deep desire to be a doctor like his father, of his fear that he would never grow big, that he was doomed to be a runt all his life. Bart listened with growing amazement and interest. Why, Eddie was a real person when you got underneath all that shell of shyness! He *liked* him! And to think that he had never before bothered to really get acquainted with his brother. He had always looked down on Eddie because he was younger and quiet and colorless.

When the two boys came into the kitchen, Mrs. Skinner looked from one bright face to the other. Bart met her gaze and flushed, remembering his hateful words to her.

"I'm sorry, Mom," he said quickly. "I didn't mean . . ."

Mrs. Skinner kissed him gently. "I know, Son. Wash your hands now. Dinner is ready."

The first chance he had that evening, Bart took his father aside. "Dad, Eddie wants, the worst way, to win something in the Kids' Fishing Derby. He ought to get some practice in."

Dr. Skinner shook his head determinedly. "I'm sorry, Bart. I can't let you take the boat out this week for any reason whatever. You've got to learn. . . ."

"I'm not asking to, Dad! Couldn't *you* maybe take him out, just for a little while, and teach him a few things? He could use my gear. Then next week, when I can use the boat again, I'll take him out."

Dr. Skinner looked at his elder son thoughtfully. "I'll try to arrange some time, Bart. Thanks for reminding me. . . . But about the gear: I'd forgotten Eddie hasn't any of his own. I think we can fix him up. Let's go down to the basement right now."

For the next hour Dr. Skinner and the two boys pawed happily through fishing gear, discussing the relative merits of each lure, testing leaders, polishing spoons and dodgers, sorting out duplicates for Eddie.

"It's a funny thing," said Dr. Skinner suddenly, apropos of nothing, looking down at the flasher in his hand, "the way boys grow."

At once Bart knew his mother had reported his rude words to his father.

"Some grow early, some grow late. Some grow to be

121

tall husky men, some remain short all their lives."

Bart and Eddie looked at each other, sharing the same thought: were they doomed to be the latter?

"You can't help your size any more than you can the color of your hair," Dr. Skinner went on, "so there's no use worrying about it. Just take it from here."

Bart felt an unprecedented wave of resentment against his father. It was all right for *him* to talk about not worrying. *He* was tall. It wasn't so easy when you were a "half-pint."

"The important thing is not how big you are on the outside," his father continued. "It's what's inside that counts."

As Bart got ready for bed that night he thought that he could not remember an evening he had enjoyed more. And yet what had he done that was so much fun? Merely helped his brother get ready for some fishing practice.

No, there was more to it than that. He had made Eddie feel that he *cared* about him, and the younger boy's response to this interest had been amazing and heart-warming. Bart knew he would never again forget that Eddie was a boy just like himself, with the very same growing-up problems. . . . Well, anyway, he would *try* not to forget.

Bart was almost asleep when he remembered his own problems. Somehow the loss of his Malt Shop job and his rivalry with Steve did not seem half as big and important now as they had this afternoon. Somehow everything would work out.

He turned over and went to sleep.

122

13. RESCUE

"LET'S STOP A WHILE AND WATCH THE pile-driver," Eddie suggested.

Bart cut the motor, and both boys took in their lines. The boat drifted with the tide, bouncing on the choppy sea.

The boys watched the men on the big barge operate the huge sledge hammer which drove posts the size of telephone poles deep into the bottom of the Sound. There was something fascinating about machinery that could handle great tree trunks as if they were matchsticks. This must be the new dock they had read about in the paper.

Bart's eyes turned to his brother, sitting opposite him in the boat. Eddie had certainly changed in these last two weeks. Still not much of a talker, his face glowed and his eyes were wide and interested—quite a contrast to his previous clammed-up expression.

Funny what a difference a little brotherly affection could make in a kid. Ever since the evening he had helped Eddie with his paper route for the first time, Bart had made it a point to devote some time to Eddie every day. At first it was mostly questions about the paper route and Eddie's school work, or challenging him to a game of catch.

Since Dr. Skinner had raised the ban on Bart's taking the boat out, the older boy had gone fishing with Eddie several times, after helping him with his paper route so he could get through in time. In return, Eddie had outdone himself trying to repay Bart by helping with his yard work and wiping the dishes. Mrs. Skinner laughed about it. "I ask for one boy to help me, and I get two! Service, I call it."

Rain began to fall in a steady drizzle. Bart started the motor. "We'd better get going, Eddie. Not too much time."

Eddie took a last lingering look at the pile-driver and started to put his line in the water. Bart noticed with satisfaction how much skill and confidence Eddie had gained in these recent fishing sessions. He was going to make a good fisherman.

"The pile-driver has stopped," Eddie observed, testing the drag on his line.

Bart nodded. "Quitting time, probably. They start early and stop early on that job."

Luck seemed to have deserted them today. Their favorite method of fishing (trolling with herring and dodger) brought no results. Spoons proved no better. Then they tried mooching, still without success. The rain increased to a genuine shower, and the wind freshened. Reluctantly Bart turned the boat in a wide circle.

"We'd better head home. Looks like we're in for a storm."

124

As the boat raced through the rain, Bart caught a glimpse of a dark speck off to the right, bobbing on the choppy waves.

"What's that? Driftwood or a boat?"

Eddie turned to look. "It's a boat—or is it?"

Bart shifted the tiller and steered for the dark speck. As the distance between them lessened, the drifting object became larger.

"If it is a boat," Eddie went on with growing excitement, "and we salvage it, then it's ours, isn't it, Bart? Then you and I would have a boat of our very own!"

"We have to report it to the Coast Guard," Bart reminded him. "If no one claims it, *then* it will be ours."

"It *is* a boat!" Eddie exclaimed a moment later, peering intently over the dark water. "The oars are still in the oarlocks. But there's no one in it!"

Instantly dreams of salvage vanished. The brothers looked soberly at each other, the same dark thought in the mind of each: oars in the oarlocks meant that the boat's occupant had fallen overboard. No one in his right mind would get out of his boat voluntarily and leave oars trailing in the water.

"Watch the water closely," Bart directed his brother. "Watch for someone in the water while I steer."

Eddie leaned over the side and strained his eyes to see in the gathering gloom of rain and dusk, and Bart sent the skiff straight for the derelict boat.

But they had still seen no sign of life by the time Bart cut the motor and drifted alongside the other craft.

The name on the side marked the derelict as a rental from

125

the boathouse. Eddie grabbed the gunwale and held on.

Bart scrambled over the side of their skiff into the other boat. Quickly he shipped the trailing oars, his keen eyes taking in the fishing rod lying in the bottom, the open tackle box, and a fair-sized salmon-trout beside them. Aside from these things, the boat was empty. There was no clue to what had happened to its occupant.

Bart made his way to the bow of the boat and picked up the end of the mooring rope. He tied the derelict for towing, and climbed back into the skiff.

"Want to run the motor, Eddie? I'll keep watch for someone in the water."

Eddie changed seats willingly, and started the motor. He handled the boat like a veteran, Bart thought. He had really learned a lot in these few fishing sessions.

The gloom was deepening fast with the early dusk of a rainy day. Bart took up his flashlight. (Never again, after his experience in the fog, would he go out fishing in the afternoon without a flashlight.) He swept the light back and forth across the boat's course. Several times he saw a black dot on the water ahead, but it always turned out to be merely driftwood.

"Listen!" cried Eddie suddenly. "Do you hear someone calling?"

The boys sat tense, listening. Across the roughening sea came a faint shout: "Help!"

Eddie turned the tiller toward the sound, and Bart saw that they were heading for a huge dark shape silhouetted against the gray water—the pile-driver barge. As they came closer, the boys could see a single figure standing on the

126

deck of the barge. Someone was marooned there!

The shout came again. "Help!" It was louder this time and clearer. There was something familiar about that voice, Bart thought.

When he heard it a third time, he was certain: the person on the barge was Steve!

At once Bart knew exactly what had happened, as surely as if he had seen the whole thing. Steve, out fishing alone,

127

practising for the Kids' Fishing Derby, had been intrigued by the pile-driver, just as he and Eddie had been. Steve had come alongside, either just as the workmen were leaving or after they had gone. He had climbed aboard the raft to get a closer look at the huge machinery, neglecting to ship his oars, and forgetting to tie his boat. When he had satisfied his curiosity about the pile-driver, he found that his boat had drifted off, out of reach. And Steve could not swim even the hundred yards between the barge and the shore!

Bart snorted in disgust. When he had said to himself that no one in his right mind would leave oars in the oarlocks, he should have added, "No one except a blunderer like Steve who doesn't know a thing about boats."

"Don't stop, Eddie," Bart directed. "Go on past."

The smaller boy, steering directly for the barge, looked at his brother in amazement. "You mean, leave him there?" His voice was incredulous.

"It won't hurt him a bit," Bart announced sharply. "He may get wet and cold and hungry, but the workmen will take him ashore when they come in the morning."

"But . . ."

"I tell you, I know who it is! It's Steve Huber. It will do him good to stay out there all night. And it will teach him a lesson that might save his life some day: not to leave his boat to drift when it should be anchored."

Reluctantly Eddie turned the boat away from the barge and headed for home.

"Besides," Bart went on, "if we are late getting in, Dad won't let us take the boat out again this week. You wouldn't like that, would you?"

128

Eddie sighed in relief. "I get it now. You're going to come back for Steve after you let Dad know where you are." His voice was full of warmth and confidence again. "I might have known you wouldn't do a dirty trick like leaving a fellow stranded."

The slight emphasis on the "you" flicked Bart's conscience like a whip. Yipes! Did Eddie really think that highly of him? Whew! That was something to think about.

Bart tried to laugh. "I—I was only joking. Good idea to let Steve think we weren't going to rescue him. Worry him a little. You can turn back now."

"I knew it!" cried Eddie triumphantly, turning the tiller. "I knew you wouldn't do a mean trick."

Bart was glad that in the dusk Eddie could not see his flush of shame. He would never let Eddie know that he had been only too ready to leave Steve on the barge for a night of loneliness and fear. Yes, it would have been a mean trick.

He turned around and yelled toward the barge. "We're coming. We're coming, Steve."

It took only a few seconds to maneuver the skiff up beside the barge. Steve dropped down in their boat, shaking with relief, almost incoherent with gratitude.

Bart cut him short. "Skip it. We'd have done the same thing for a dog."

129

14. THE DERBY RALLY

BART AND EDDIE HAD NOT BEEN IN THE house ten minutes when the storm broke. Rain pelted the windows. Wind shrieked and wailed and shook the very foundation.

Bart turned on the yard lights. He loved to watch the Sound during a storm, especially at high tide like this.

Outside, in the pale circle of the yard lights, a tremendous wave dashed against the bulkhead, sending its white spray high in the air. Beyond, scattered on the black water, the foam of whitecaps gleamed with a ghostly light. Another wave hit the bulkhead, then another, seeming to vent their fury against the wall of cement which stood in their path. The wind blew the salt spray against the window, obscuring Bart's view.

He turned away, to find Eddie standing beside him. So Eddie, too, loved to watch a storm. How many things they had in common that Bart had never dreamed of!

"We got in just in time," he remarked.

130

Eddie nodded. "Wonder if Steve made it."

"Sure. He only had a block to go."

For three days the storm raged, making fishing impossible. Bart's early pleasure in the wildness of the water and the wind diminished rapidly, swallowed up in the growing worry that it would not stop by Saturday, and Saturday was to be the big day: the day of the Harbor City Kids' Fishing Derby. If the storm continued, the Derby would be canceled; no boats would be allowed to go out on the bay in weather like this.

On Thursday evening, the night of the traditional Derby Rally, the storm had not abated a single bit. If anything, the wind had increased in fury, and the rain fell thicker and faster than ever. Bart grew gloomier by the minute, not only because he feared the Derby might be called off, but because he had still not made up his quarrel with Vic. Every year since they had been old enough to fish in the Kids' Derby, Bart and Vic had gone together to the Rally. Every year they had fished together. But this year . . . Bart wanted, the worst way, to call Vic and ask if they couldn't be friends again, but he didn't quite have the nerve to say he was sorry.

At seven o'clock the doorbell rang. Bart went to the door.

"Vic!" All of his fondness for Vic and his anxiety to make up their quarrel went into Bart's voice.

"Hi!"

For a minute they just stood and looked at each other, smiling uncertainly. Then Bart, collecting his senses, cried, "Come in! Come out of the rain."

131

Vic stepped into the entry, shaking the water from his cap. "You about ready to go to the rally?"

Bart could hardly speak for gratitude. Vic wasn't going to make him apologize, or make any explanations, or anything. They would go to the rally together as usual, and everything would be the same as always. Good old Vic!

The three boys, Bart, Vic and Eddie, walked down to Harbor Park for the rally, fighting the wind at every step. They did not talk much on the way, partly because the wind whipped the words out of their mouths and flung them out to sea, but mostly because they kept wondering if the rally was really a waste of time. Would there be a Fishing Derby, after all?

In spite of the weather and the general pessimism about the Derby, the recreation hall overflowed with prospective contestants. It seemed to Bart that every boy and girl in Harbor City had crowded into the room. There were some who were obviously too young to enter the Derby. They had come along with older brothers and sisters just to share in the excitement. And there were some, past fifteen, who had fished in their last Derby, but who wanted to taste again, vicariously, the fun of the contest.

Each contestant, as he entered the huge hall, was given a ticket for the door prize drawing. Sometimes, the three boys knew, the door prizes were almost as nice as the lesser prizes for the Derby itself. They put their ticket stubs carefully in their pockets until time for the drawing.

A gleaming bicycle leaned against the platform at the front of the room, a beautiful racing job.

"Boy!" cried Eddie, his eyes on this top prize. The word

was full of the awe and longing he could not express.

Bart examined the bicycle carefully. What a beauty! All red and silver. Hand brakes. Generator lights. Even a horn.

Vic put Bart's thought into words. "That's the finest prize they have ever given in this Fishing Derby. The fellow who gets it will be mighty lucky."

Bart nodded vigorous agreement. Mighty lucky, indeed —and he intended to be that lucky fellow.

Eddie had little hope of winning the bicycle. He turned to look at the remainder of the prizes displayed on the platform. Bart and Vic followed suit.

Second prize, a camera with flash attachment. Third prize, a portable radio. Fourth, a sleeping bag. Fifth, a tennis racquet. Sixth, a genuine leather notebook. Seventh . . .

The seventh prize was concealed from view in a big, carefully wrapped box. By tradition, "Lucky Seven" was something special, and always a surprise, known only to the committee member in charge of prizes and to the merchant who had donated it. What could it be?

"Lucky Seven," said Eddie wistfully. Shyly he added, "I'd like to get that." Quickly he glanced at Bart, afraid he might scoff.

But Bart nodded matter-of-factly. "Maybe you will. You have as good a chance as anybody."

Eddie beamed.

Soon Bart stirred uneasily. The crowd pressing around the platform to see the prizes had become overpowering to him. He always felt small and insignificant with people towering over him on all sides. Even though half of this mob of kids was no bigger than he . . .

"Let's get out of here," he said. "You lead, Eddie. Find some seats."

Surprisingly, Eddie objected. "No, *you* lead, Bart. I'll follow *you*."

As Bart threaded his way through the press of boisterous young people, he pondered Eddie's last remark. Was it his imagination, Bart wondered, or did his kid brother's words hold a hint of a promise? Could Eddie mean he wanted to *be like* him?

Suddenly the meaning of dozens of tiny incidents of the past two weeks became clear: Eddie in front of the mirror, combing his hair like Bart's. Eddie asking his mother for shoes like Bart's. Eddie trying a fumbling wise-crack at the dinner table. No doubt about it, Eddie had taken Bart as his model!

Whew! Bart whistled soundlessly. If his kid brother was going to copy him, he would have to watch his step.

"Here's three seats," said Vic.

As they settled down in their seats, the big hall rang with the excited shouts and laughter of a hundred and fifty children, but Bart did not add his voice to the uproar. If Eddie was going to copy him, he had to set a good example.

Vic began to talk to the boy on the other side of him. Eddie sat, absorbed in his thoughts, a far-away look in his eyes.

Two rows in front of them, Bart saw Steve and Lexy, side by side. Lexy's face, turned toward her companion, was vivacious and glowing. He could hear Steve's booming voice, but he could not make out the words. All at

134

once resentment and jealousy of Steve swept over Bart again in an overpowering rush. He had to beat Steve in this Derby. He *had* to!

"I've got to do it," he said to himself. "I've simply *got* to!"

"What did you say, Bart?" asked Eddie.

Bart flushed. He must have spoken aloud. "Nothing. I was just thinking."

But Eddie's question had turned his mind away from his own disquieting thoughts. He looked at his young brother. Although Eddie sat quietly and took no part in the whistling and screaming which served as an outlet for the excitement of most of the crowd, he was as thrilled as any of the others—as thrilled as if this were his first Derby.

Suddenly Bart realized why. This was the first year Eddie had felt he had a chance to win anything. It was the first time he had felt any confidence in his fishing ability.

And he himself, Bart knew, was largely responsible for his brother's new-found confidence. The knowledge gave him a good warm feeling. Maybe Eddie would not win anything—luck played a big part in fishing, after all. But know-how had a lot to do with it, too, so he stood a good chance.

The chairman rapped for order. His gavel made no impression on the uproar.

Crazy kids, Bart thought. Couldn't they see how childishly they were acting? Yet only last year, he remembered with a start, he had been one of the last ones to simmer down at the rally.

135

The chairman leaned close to the microphone. "QUIET!" he bellowed. The noise stopped as if cut off with a knife.

"That's better." The chairman smiled. "We have a good program for you kids tonight, and some mighty fine door prizes. But first I want you to meet the people who have put in a lot of time organizing this thirteenth annual Harbor City Kids' Fishing Derby. General chairman of the Derby this year is Mr. Jensen. . . ."

Bart paid little attention to the introductions. He knew all these men. His father should have been there to be introduced, too, but as usual he had been called out on a case. If only he didn't have an emergency call Saturday morning!

"Now we have Mr. Boone, principal of Harbor High, who has a few words to say to you. Mr. Boone has worked with young people for many years. During the summers he coaches tennis teams and swimming teams, and he is a fisherman of considerable note. Last year he won the Puget Sound Fishing Derby, which, as you all know, is the biggest derby in this part of the country."

Bart scowled. Why did they have to get old Boone-goon down here? He certainly didn't want to listen to him lecture. But Mr. Boone's first words caught his attention.

"How many of you want to win this bicycle?"

Every hand in the hall went up. "How many of you would like to have this little loving cup which the committee will present to the best fisherman?" He held up a tiny shining trophy.

Again the hands waved in the air.

"Well, only one boy or girl can win the bicycle, and

only one can get this cup. But each of you can win in another way."

Mr. Boone paused. The room was quiet now, as boys and girls alike puzzled over his meaning.

"In every contest, in every race, in every football or basketball game or tennis match, you are competing with other people. But at the same time another contest is taking place, and it is a much more important contest. You are competing *against yourself*."

Again he paused. Not a whisper in the big room.

"Each of you is two people, really. Part of you wants to win at any cost. You want to win that bike. You want to get this cup. You want to beat everyone else, no matter how you do it.

"But another part of you (sometimes you call it your conscience) isn't nearly as interested in the winning and the prize as it is in something else: it is interested in the kind of person you are, and the kind of man or woman you are going to be when you grow up. So it reminds you of the rules when you are tempted to do something you know is wrong. It reminds you that other people have feelings, too, when you are tempted to be selfish or angry. That other part of you wants you to be a good sport, whether you win or lose. And if you are a good sport in this Fishing Derby, then you have won the most important contest of all, even if you don't get a single prize."

Bart scowled. The same old line. It isn't *whether* you win, but *how* you win that counts. He might have known old Boone would talk like that, instead of giving them some good pointers on fishing that might help them on

Saturday.

Hands in his pockets, Bart jingled his change impatiently. Eddie turned to look at him inquiringly.

Again Bart became aware that he was being used as a model. He took his hands out of his pockets and straightened up to listen courteously to Mr. Boone's closing remarks.

". . . so good fishing and good sportsmanship to all of you! Thank you." Mr. Boone left the platform amid lukewarm applause.

A short movie followed. It pictured the life cycle of the salmon. The three boys watched it with rapt attention. Funny how a salmon could tell the stream where it was born and go up that very stream to spawn and die. . . .

The rally continued. The rules of the Derby were read and explained.

"Fishing boundaries: between the Lighthouse on the west and the boathouse on the east. Starting gun at six A. M. and closing gun at ten. Contestants must be accompanied by an adult unless they have permission to fish alone. Contestants may have help in netting their fish, but they must hook and play them alone; no adult may touch a contestant's rod. All fish must be at the weighing station at the finish signal."

Bart knew all the rules by heart. He listened only to be certain nothing new had been added. But everything was the same as last year—everything except that this year Barton Skinner would be the top prize winner!

A question period followed the reading of the rules.

Fully half the contestants, it seemed to Bart, had a question to ask.

"How can we tell if the fish we catch is under the legal length?"

"When you check in at the Derby," the chairman answered, "you will be given a number tag to wear. That tag will be twelve inches long, which is the minimum length for salmon."

"What do we do with a fish that's too small?"

Bart sniffed. What a stupid question! Any dope knew the answer to that. Throw it back in, of course!

"What if we catch a cod or a sole?"

"Keep it," came the prompt response. "Prizes will be awarded to salmon first, on the basis of weight. But if we have more prizes than there are salmon caught (and that has happened in at least two Derbies) the remaining prizes will be given for the largest cod, sole, dog-fish, etc."

"May we use motorboats?"

The chairman sighed. So many of these questions had already been answered. "If you had listened to the reading of the rules, you would know. You may use *any* kind of boat you want—even a freighter, I guess, if you can hire one!"

The girls giggled, the boys whistled and shouted. The chairman decided that the question period was over, and he went on to the drawing for the door prizes.

The doorman brought up his big box, in which each contestant had put his ticket stub. The smallest child in the audience was chosen to do the drawing.

139

The first door prize was a shining new reel.

"235–897," the chairman called out.

Bart and his companions looked at their tickets and shook their heads regretfully.

Ahead of them Steve bellowed, "That's me!"

He lumbered into the aisle, stepping on everyone's toes, and dashed to the platform, leaving a chorus of wails behind him. He carried the reel back to his seat, gazing at it as proudly as if it were made of solid gold.

The second prize, a pocket compass, was won by one of Eddie's classmates.

The third prize, a bill-fold, went to a stranger.

The last door-prize was a flasher. Lexy held the winning ticket this time. Bart watched her walk lightly up the aisle, smile her thanks to the chairman, and come back to her seat.

For the first time she saw Bart sitting behind her.

"Why, Barton Skinner!" she exclaimed. "Where did you come from? I didn't know you were here."

"Been sitting right here behind you all evening," he assured her breezily.

"But I can't believe it! I didn't hear you. I mean, you haven't been . . . That is, you didn't . . ." She gave it up, shrugged and sat down. "Well, it's nice to see you."

Bart slid farther down in his seat. Now what on earth was the matter with Lexy? Why was she so incredulous to find him there?

It was not until the rally was over and the boys were home again that Bart realized something that might explain Lexy's surprise. Although at the rally he had been, as usual, a runt lost in a crowd, he had made no move to get attention. Conscious of Eddie's possible imitation, he had not done a single solitary show-off thing. Was that what Lexy meant? Was that why she was surprised?

15. READY FOR THE BIG DAY

BART WOKE THE NEXT MORNING TO THE happy consciousness that the storm had either worn itself out or passed on to new territory. At any rate, the wind had died to a whisper, and the rain had slowed to a mere drizzle.

During breakfast he turned on the radio weather report. "Partly cloudy, light winds west to southwest . . ." Good! They could expect decent weather for the Derby tomorrow. Some rain, perhaps, but who cared about that as long as the Sound was not rough?

All day long, one topic of conversation prevailed all over Harbor City. At home, at school, downtown, on the bus—the Kids' Fishing Derby dominated every gathering.

As the students got on the bus, the driver asked with a grin, "Who's going to win the bicycle?" And he laughed good-naturedly at the chorus of "I am's" which greeted the query.

At school, teachers smiled tolerantly at the bubbling enthusiasm the students brought to each class. Most instructors took advantage of tomorrow's Derby to add interest to their assignments. The mathematics teacher posed problems like this one: "If a salmon fifteen inches long weighs five pounds, and a salmon twenty inches long weighs ten pounds, what should be the weight of a salmon thirty inches long?"

The English teacher had her classes write extemporaneous compositions on the subject, "Why I Like To Fish In the Harbor City Kids' Fishing Derby."

The biology professor conducted discussions on the life and habits of the salmon. Even the Latin instructor concentrated on vocabulary connected with fish and the sea. Only the history teacher ignored the coming event and concentrated on affairs of the past.

Bart went from class to class, happy and excited, too full of thoughts about tomorrow's fun and possible triumph to do any showing-off today. Although he attracted no attention in English class, he felt pleasantly conscious, as he handed in his composition, that he had stated clearly and sincerely his honest enthusiasm for the annual Fishing Derby. Although he got no laughs in biology class, his fund of information about salmon and salmon fishing won him respectful glances from his classmates and commendation from his teacher.

When school was over, Bart went to the barber shop for a haircut. He wanted to look nice in the pictures the newspapers would take of him with his winning fish and the prize bicycle. Then he hurried home. He would get all of his stuff ready for tomorrow morning as quickly as possible, so that he could help take the boats down to Harbor Park after dinner.

A note on the kitchen door told him his mother had gone down to the park to work on food preparation for the Derby.

Bart went down to the basement. He had begun to go through his tackle box, checking to be certain everything was in order, when he remembered Eddie. The kid, too, should organize his gear, and waterproof his jeans and his boots, and collect his wool socks and the rest of his clothes. But it would take Eddie so long to do his paper route alone that he would have little time for anything else before dinner. Oh, well, that was Eddie's hard luck. Bart had helped him often enough lately with his paper route. Eddie could hardly expect assistance again today.

Bart held his pet flasher to the light, to see if it needed polishing. But Eddie's face came between, and he seemed to hear the kid's voice saying, "I'll follow *you*."

Rats! He couldn't let Eddie follow him in selfishness. Bart tossed the flasher back in the tackle box and shut the lid. Might as well go and help Eddie. Then they could work together getting ready for tomorrow. He raced out the basement door and up the driveway.

Dinner was a gala affair that evening. Bart and Eddie laughed and chattered, and exchanged frequent glances, happy in the knowledge that both of them had everything ready for the call of the alarm clock tomorrow morning. Dr. Skinner teased and joked like a boy, and Mrs. Skinner smiled around the table at her "men-folks."

144

"I declare, Eddie," she said cheerfully, "you're getting to be just like Bart. You talk all the time."

Eddie grinned as if that were high praise, and Bart smiled self-consciously. It was nice to know that his kid brother admired him and looked up to him, but it was a big responsibility, too.

It had been arranged that Bart and Vic would fish together in the Derby as usual, using the outboard motor, and Dr. Skinner would take Eddie and another younger boy in Vic's rowboat. Bart and his father and Vic had planned to tow the Jensen boat and Vic's down to Harbor Park beach tonight while Mr. Jensen and Vic's father worked on last-minute business details of the Derby.

"Do you boys think you could take the boats down tonight without me?" Dr. Skinner asked. "If I am to take time to go out with Eddie in the Derby tomorrow, I must check on a couple of patients tonight. I'll be down in time to bring the motor back, probably about nine-thirty."

"Why, sure," Bart answered promptly. "We can do it, Dad."

Mrs. Skinner refused to let Eddie accompany the older boys. He must get to bed early, she insisted, to be ready for the long, exciting day ahead of him.

Bart and Vic got the three boats in the water and tied them securely, bow to stern. Then they put the motor on the lead boat and set off in the darkness. Bart steered, while Vic beamed his flashlight on the water ahead of them.

Progress was slow. With the weight of the following boats, Bart could not have speeded much if he had wanted to. Besides, with only a flashlight to illuminate their course, he knew it was important to steer cautiously through the moonless night.

Floodlights, added to the regular lights along the Promenade, made Harbor Park almost as light as day. The beach crawled with dark figures when the boys reached it with their little train of boats. Many others in Harbor City, who intended to use their own boats in tomorrow's Derby, were bringing them down tonight, so as to save half an hour's time in the morning.

Bart and Vic pulled their craft, one at a time, up on the beach, well above high tide mark. As they went back for the third boat Vic asked, "Shall we take the motor off and set it up by the street, ready for your father?"

Bart hesitated. "I don't know. Dad's house calls may take twice as long as he expected. . . ."

While they stood, debating, Mr. Jensen came out of the recreation hall.

"Oh, Bart! Got your motor?"

"Yes, sir."

"The boats haven't come yet from the boathouse."

The boys understood the reason for Mr. Jensen's worried frown. Most of tomorrow's young fishermen did not have boats of their own. They counted on using boats from Harbor Boathouse. The manager had promised sixty boats to the Derby, and they must be brought down tonight.

"I wonder . . ." Mr. Jensen looked down at Bart. "Could you boys help ferry some of the boats from the boathouse? The tug that was supposed to bring them has been held up on a towing job. We'll have to tow them down ourselves, a few at a time."

146

Bart and Vic looked at each other and nodded. "Sure!"

"How many can you bring?"

"Five or six, probably. Wouldn't make much time, but . . ."

Mr. Jensen nodded. "Fine." He gave the boys the name of the man at the boathouse to speak to, tossed them a coil of rope, and went on to round up others with out-

147

board motors who could help.

By the time that Bart and Vic had made two trips to the boathouse and back (maddeningly slow coming back with six boats trailing behind), they were very tired.

"Any more?" Vic called, as the shore crew took over their string of boats.

"One more trip ought to do it."

"Okay."

It was Bart's turn to handle the boat. When the rope had been tossed back to them, he turned the tiller and headed toward the boathouse, opening the throttle wide.

"At least you can pep it up a little," he said, "when you aren't hauling a string of boats."

The lights along the promenade illuminated the water, so that steering was not difficult, but the hour was growing late and the boys weary. They would be glad to see the end of this task.

They met five or six strings of boats between the park and the boathouse, all plugging along slowly and patiently. When the skiff coasted up to the boathouse, the proprietor held up his hands and grinned. "That's all there is, kids. There ain't any more."

"Yippee!" cried Bart. No poking along on the return trip this time. He could go as fast as he wanted. He swung the boat in a circle and took off after the last string of boats. He kept to starboard of the string until he had barely passed the lead boat. Then he cut sharply across her bow, to zoom up the port side of the string ahead. When he cut across the bow of that lead boat, to skim along the starboard side of the next string, Vic spoke.

148

"What's got into you, Bart? I thought you were through with that show-off stuff."

For a moment Bart's anger flared. Who did Vic think he was, telling him how to act?

Immediately, however, his better judgment came to his rescue. It *was* show-off stuff, and dangerous, too. If he should misjudge, in the half-light, which boat was the lead, and try to cut over between two tows, he would hit the rope at full tilt. No telling what might happen, what damage might be done.

"Sorry," he said briefly, and steered a safe and sane course for the park beach.

"There's your dad," Vic observed as the skiff grounded. Bart looked up to see the tall, familiar figure coming down to the shore. The boys beached their boat and unscrewed the motor. They loaded it in the doctor's car, glad that the ferrying job was done.

In a few minutes they were home again, dog-tired, but happy in the prospects of a great day tomorrow.

16. THE START

BART HALF ROUSED FROM A DEEP, DREAM-less sleep. His room was pitch black. Furtive movements in the room next to his suggested that his parents were up. What could be the trouble?

Then his eyes sprang wide open. This was Derby Day!

Sleepiness disappeared on the instant. Bart sprang out of bed. No time to waste this morning. He wanted to be down at the park well ahead of the starting gun. He went to rouse Eddie.

By the time the boys, looking rather bulky with their extra layers of warm clothes, entered the breakfast nook, Mrs. Skinner had a man-sized breakfast ready: fruit, hot cereal, bacon and eggs, toast, cocoa and coffee. Bart stowed away a hearty meal, but Eddie was too excited to eat much, in spite of his mother's anxious urgings.

"Let him alone," said Dr. Skinner. "We'll take a few sandwiches along, and some fruit, in case he gets hungry."

There was a last minute checking to be sure each fisher-

150

man had gloves, warm cap, rain poncho, rod and reel and tackle. Then the family hurried outside to get in the car.

Bart took stock of the weather. No wind. A light drizzle. Not too cold. Perfect fishing weather. He nodded in satisfaction and climbed in the car beside his brother.

It was early yet; they would be among the first arrivals. The wet streets were still deserted, although lights showed in many of the houses they passed. In another hour this street would have almost as much traffic as it normally did in midmorning.

Dr. Skinner parked the car in front of the recreation hall. Bart and Eddie jumped out and ran to get the motor out of the trunk. As quickly as if they were late, in place of three-quarters of an hour early, the boys hastened to take their gear down to the beach.

While Eddie and his father got their boat, Bart pulled the skiff down to the water's edge and fastened the motor on it. Boats could not be launched until the starting gun, but he could have everything prepared. He stowed his tackle neatly, attached his reel to his rod, and checked over everything carefully with the aid of his flashlight, to be sure all was in readiness.

Why didn't Vic come? If he was late, and delayed their start . . . But it couldn't be more than 5:30. He had plenty of time. Vic was slow-moving, but he was seldom late.

Boat and gear ready, Bart went up on the park promenade, which was again illuminated by floodlights. Early as it was, the place swarmed with people and more were coming all the time. Wide-eyed ten-year-olds in raincoats

151

and rubber boots, out for their first Derby. Girls in slacks and slickers, their heads swathed in bandanas. Older boys, for whom today would be the last Kids' Derby. Men in hunting togs, women in camping clothes. Everyone busy and excited.

A small group of children clustered around the bait bin, waiting for their share of herring. Bart joined them; he had brought his own bait, but Vic might forget.

Mr. Boone presided over the bait bin. When Bart's turn came, the high school principal handed the boy a paper cup full of small herring, with scarcely a glance at him.

"Eight to a fisherman," he said. "And no seconds."

As Bart carried the bait down to his boat, he saw Steve hurrying up toward the promenade. Armed with rod and reel and a shiny new tackle box, the big fellow stumbled over his own feet in his eagerness.

"Hi, Bart!"

"Hi!" Bart started on, but Steve called after him.

"What do I do?"

Bart turned back. "Get your bait and check in." He motioned to the table, pushed under the eaves of the recreation hall in a vain attempt to get it out of the rain. Two women (one of them Mrs. Skinner) checked off the names of the fishermen and gave out their entry tags. Steve nodded and turned toward the table.

That reminded Bart that he, himself, had not yet checked in. He set the cup of herring in his boat and returned to the registration table, just as Vic came up.

The two boys joined the line of registrants, which had doubled in the few minutes since Bart first noticed it.

"Got everything?" Bart asked his partner.

"I think so," answered Vic.

A loud voice startled them.

"Testing. Testing."

It was just the men hooking up the loud-speaker. Soon they would begin giving directions to the crowd, which was swelling fast. The line of fishermen extended clear around the corner of the recreation hall now. Men milled about on the promenade, some of them with definite jobs to do, others merely waiting until it was time to take their sons or daughters out fishing. Most of the women who stood around were warmly dressed in slacks and heavy shoes and parkas or waterproofed jackets, but others wore incongruous open-toed slippers and dresses topped by long coats.

The black of the sky had given way to gray. The harbor showed dull slate gray against the lightening sky.

"Attention, please." It was Mr. Jensen's voice on the loud-speaker. "All contestants must check in at the registration desk before beginning to fish. Repeat: even if you have your own boat, *you must register!*"

Bart had now reached the head of the line.

"Name, please?" asked his mother without looking up.

"Barton Skinner."

She glanced up at him and smiled. "Oh, it's you, Bart." She turned her flashlight down on the list and checked off his name, while her companion handed him a tag, twelve inches long, marked with the number "33."

"Do you need a boat?" Mrs. Skinner asked automatically, then caught herself with a little laugh. "Of course not. You

153

have your own boat. Who is going out with you?"

"Vic."

"Yes, of course. And you don't need an adult, do you? Next."

Bart stepped aside to let Vic up to the table, and pinned on his number tag. He had really intended to be the first to register so he would get number "1," but he had forgotten it in his hurry to get his boat and gear ready. Oh, well, the number didn't matter. It was the fish you caught.

The crowd on the promenade now took on the aspects of a mob, everyone hurrying, loud and excited. The loudspeaker blared again: "Do not launch your boat until the starting signal. Repeat: *Do not* launch your boat until the shot is fired. Ten minutes yet."

Bart looked around. He had not seen Eddie or his father since their arrival. . . . There they were, down at their boat, all set to go. How little Eddie looked! But he was a better fisherman than lots of the big fellows. Bart hoped his kid brother would catch a big enough fish to get a good prize.

Vic had finished registering. He pinned on his tag, number "34," and the two boys hurried down to wait beside their boat.

"Five minutes." It was Mr. Jensen on the microphone again. "Remember, contestants, no boat is allowed to go beyond the boundary limits, which are the lighthouse on the west, and the boathouse on the east, and no fisherman is to go out in the bay farther than the Harbor Patrol boats on the north boundary.

"If you need a boat, or someone to take you out, report

154

*All along the beach boats were lined up, a hundred at least,
most of them flanked by impatient contestants.*

here at the microphone."

Bart and Vic stood by the stern of their boat, waiting for the signal to push it into the water. All along the beach boats were lined up, a hundred at least, most of them flanked by impatient contestants.

"Three minutes."

There was Lexy, down the shore. Who was she going out with? Her father, as chairman of the Derby, could not leave the loud-speaker to take her fishing today.

Then Bart scowled as he saw a big lumbering figure join Lexy. Steve! She was fishing with Steve today!

Bart tried to tell himself he didn't care. Lexy would be sorry. Steve would be no help to her in baiting her hooks or landing her fish—if she caught one; he would do well to take care of his own gear. It served Lexy right, Bart thought. If she had not been so snooty, he might have taken her with him, in place of Vic.

"Two minutes." Bart caught his breath. "You all know the rules, contestants. Any infringement of rules, remember, will disqualify your fish."

Activity on the promenade became more hectic. It was organized bedlam now. Late arrivals dashed up, pushing their way through the mob of on-lookers to the registration desk.

"One minute."

Bart and Vic grinned at each other. With one accord they bent over and took hold of the stern of the boat. Bart forgot Lexy and Steve, he forgot Eddie, he forgot his own determination to win top prize. All he could think of was the pleasurable excitement of this moment, waiting for the gun, with every muscle tensed.

"Ready!"

The sound of a shot exploded through the dawn. Bart and Vic gave their boat a tremendous shove and clambered aboard. The Fishing Derby had begun.

17. OUT TO WIN

VIC GRABBED UP AN OAR AND BEGAN TO push the boat into deep water, while Bart turned his attention to the motor.

For a minute he was too busy to notice how the other contestants around him were doing. The motor proved stubborn. It took half a dozen tries to get the thing started.

At last the engine caught. Its welcome *"put-put"* increased in tempo. Vic stowed the oar away carefully, and Bart snatched the tiller and guided the craft skillfully through the maze of rowboats out into open water.

Safely past the slower boats, Bart looked back on the scene at the beach. It was growing lighter every minute. Late-comers were still launching their craft. In close to shore the boats were so thick the oarsmen had trouble finding room to row. Bart was thankful his father had let him take the motor, so he and Vic could get a good start.

The voice over the loud-speaker echoed across the water:

"We need a few more adults to go out with some kids. If you are willing to take a kid fishing, report here at the mike. Repeat: we need more men—or women—who can handle a boat."

Bart cut the motor to trolling speed. The boys baited their hooks and let out their lines, glad that they had mounted their reels and rigged their lines while waiting for the starting gun. They had begun to fish before the main body of contestants had reached water open enough to risk dropping a line.

Bart held his thumb against his reel. Yes, just the right amount of pull. Just the proper rhythmic throb which meant his bait was swerving from side to side like a live herring.

From the center seat of the boat Vic looked at him questioningly. "Okay?"

Bart nodded. "Okay. You, too?"

"Perfect. Now if we just have some luck . . ."

Overhead a flock of geese, black against the sky, flew south in V-shaped formation. Bart watched them admiringly, although rain fell in his upturned face. A beautiful sight. A beautiful day for fishing, even if it was a little wet and a bit cold.

Suddenly the significance of the V-shape struck him. "V" for victory! It was a good sign.

"We ought to have luck," he said. "We're one of the first boats out."

There were not more than a dozen outboard motors in the crowd. A couple of small cruisers were moving far out near the Harbor Patrol boat, including Parker's. One sailboat flitted along. All the rest were rowboats.

It was colder out here on the bay than Bart had anticipated. He put on his parka over his zipper-jacket and Vic pulled a poncho over his head.

A tugboat, pulling a log-boom, made its slow, unswerving way right through the Fishing Derby grounds. A couple of fishermen in a rowboat took advantage of it to get trolling speed without effort. Looping their mooring rope around the "boomstick," the outer log of the boom, they rested on their oars and took life easy.

Here and there a net, sticking up in a boat, looked like a butterfly net. Bart smiled. He'd like to see somebody chasing butterflies in a rowboat!

He changed the speed of the motor to vary the depth of their lures. Maybe the fish were near the bottom this morning.

They were opposite the boathouse now, the eastern boundary of the Derby. Bart turned the skiff and steered west.

Around the recreation hall, on the beach, people continued to scurry to and fro. Boats were still being launched as more young fishermen arrived. Behind the recreation hall rose the hill on which the main part of town was situated; it was silhouetted against the sky, dark and sleeping. There was no sign of life or light anywhere in Harbor City except at Fishing Derby headquarters, where half the town's inhabitants had congregated.

The loud-speaker sounded again, fainter now, but still audible. "Anybody got an extra sheer pin for a 3-horse Johnson?"

160

Bart caught Vic's inquiring gaze. He had an extra, but they might need it if they should run into a submerged log and break their sheer pin. "They might as well row as us," he said defensively, and Vic nodded reluctant agreement. "Anyway, they should have brought a spare."

"Does anybody afloat have room for another fisherman?" asked the loud-speaker. "If you have room for another boy, please come in to shore."

Most of the rowboats were well out in the harbor now. Boats of every size, every color, dotted the water in all directions. The rain had stopped, so quietly Bart had not noticed. Streaks of pink showed in the eastern sky. At once the bright colors of the fishermen's clothes, particularly the girls' head-scarves, deepened in hue. A ferry, passing beyond the limits of the Derby, reflected the light of the cautious sunrise.

The minutes passed slowly. Would the fish never bite? Both boys reeled in and examined their bait, then put their lines out again, twenty pulls of line. No signs of activity as yet in any of the boats around them. Was this going to be one of those Derbies, rare in Harbor City and never forgotten, where practically no fish were caught?

Bart and Vic were almost to the lighthouse. Its light was still blinking, sweeping the water in a huge circle. On the beach, a couple of men were digging clams.

Ahead, Bart saw one of the cruisers, fishing rods protruding from its deck. It reached the lighthouse point, but did not turn back.

"Look at those fellows!" Bart cried indignantly. "They're outside the boundaries!"

161

"And they've got a strike!" Vic exclaimed.

Both boys forgot their own lines and watched the furious activity in the cruiser. Bart turned their skiff to stay within the Derby limits, but he kept circling so they could watch the other fishermen.

"He's got it!" Vic exclaimed at last. "But it shouldn't count."

Bart nodded crossly. They ought to report the guys. Breaking the rules . . .

Then he noticed his own line, and thoughts of unfair play left his mind. He had a strike! And it was a big one!

Vic reeled in quickly, without being told. An experienced fisherman, he knew the danger of fouling a companion's line.

But some kids in the boat behind them were not so co-operative. Before Bart had time to realize the danger, his fish had tangled with a trailing line. At once Bart's line went slack. The fish had got away.

For an instant Bart was too furious to speak. He glared at the occupants of the other boat. They were two little children wearing life-jackets—ten-year-olds, without a doubt—accompanied by a man who held the oars as if he didn't know what they were for.

"Did you get a fish?" asked one of the children.

Bart exploded. "He got away, thanks to you! Don't you know you're supposed to reel in your line when someone near you hooks a fish?"

All three occupants of the rowboat shook their heads. "I'm sorry," the man said. "This is the first time we've ever been fishing."

162

Bart mastered his anger and managed to mutter, "That's okay. I'll get another one."

He speeded up the motor and headed out in the bay. Get away from these greenhorns where a guy would have a chance. Follow the outer boundary where there were fewer boats.

Thinking of boundaries reminded him of the cruiser and its unlawful catch. If other people could get away with it, why couldn't he and Vic go beyond the lighthouse where the fishing would undoubtedly be better?

But Bart quickly dismissed that idea. No, he just had to play fair, he knew, no matter how much he might be tempted not to.

A patrol boat had left its post on the north boundary and was heading for the lighthouse point. As Bart cut the motor down to trolling speed again, he wondered what was up. He opened his tackle box and began to string a new leader on his line. Vic let his line out and watched the patrol boat curiously.

"They saw him!" he exclaimed.

"Saw who?" asked Bart absently.

"The guy who caught the fish beyond the lighthouse. They are making him give it up. The fellow might have known it wouldn't pay to cheat."

Their lines in the water again, the boys leaned back in their seats. Vic got out a packet of sandwiches and offered one to Bart. The sun burst over the hill as if it had suddenly taken courage from its conquest of the rain. Across the Sound the Olympics loomed up underneath an overhanging bank of clouds. The light from the lighthouse stopped

163

shining abruptly.

The swells from the ferry reached them now. Bart turned the bow of the boat to cut across them.

Although they had been quite alone when they first came to this portion of the fishing grounds, now several other boats approached. Suddenly, not far from them, a girl shrieked, "I've got one, Daddy!"

"Careful, Darleen," shouted the man at the oars. "Hold tight!"

Bart guided his skiff out of her vicinity. If they got far enough away, they would not have to reel in and waste precious fishing time. He headed east, careful not to get so far out that they would be breaking rules.

Gulls screamed overhead. The motor purred softly and smoothly. Little waves slapped on the bow of the boat. Bart forgot his disappointment in losing his fish (it had been a big one, he was sure) and gave himself up to the joy of moving slowly along on the smooth water, with a beautiful day dawning overhead, and at least three hours of fishing before him. Anything could happen in three hours.

"Yippee! A strike!"

Vic clutched his rod firmly. Quickly Bart cranked in his own line, and speeded up the motor to follow the fish on its run, prepared to help Vic in his fight.

The fight did not amount to much, after all. A small salmon trout, not much over the legal limit. He gave up with scarcely a struggle. In a very few minutes Vic had netted him.

Bart turned the skiff toward shore. They would take

164

Vic's fish in to be weighed immediately, for fish lose weight after they are out of the water. Sometimes a few ounces could make a difference in the prize you won.

As they approached their previous position, they saw that the little girl was still playing her fish—and having plenty of trouble. Suddenly her father snatched the pole from her and began to reel in.

Bart and Vic exchanged glances. It was strictly against the rules for any adult to handle the rod. By his action, the man had disqualified his daughter's fish.

Unaccountably Bart's motor sputtered and then died. All around them, voices—which had been smothered in the motor's busy *"put-put"*—rose suddenly, loud and clear.

"Get some oars!" a man called waggishly over the confusion of conversation from a dozen boats.

Bart bent over the engine, checking gas and spark plugs.

"He's playing the fish for her," Vic reported. Bart did not look up, but he knew to whom Vic's pronouns referred. He could hear the girl squealing in high excitement. Then the man's voice said, "There you are, Darleen."

"He landed it," said Vic.

Bart tried the motor again. It started without protest this time, and chattered loudly, carrying them through the water as if its sudden stop had been a mere whim which it had now forgotten.

When the motor no longer needed his attention, Bart looked at Vic again, to find his friend's eyes regarding him questioningly.

"Will you tell?" asked Vic slowly.

Bart hesitated. He remembered the shining thrill in the

child's face. "I don't know. They shouldn't get by with it. . . . But the girl is so little. Her first Derby, I'll bet."

Vic nodded. "It wasn't her fault. Her father had no business grabbing her rod. Too bad to make her lose out."

Bart guided the boat onto the shore in front of the promenade and jumped out, pondering on the luck of those who broke rules, while he followed the rules conscientiously . . . and had no luck at all.

18. LUCK AT LAST

BART FOLLOWED VIC AROUND THE CORNER
of the recreation hall to the scales. Along the east side of
the building, the men had built a platform for the prizes
and the speaker, and they had improvised long counters
to display the fish. At the far end of the counters, the
official scales stood on a table. Vic trotted over to them
with his little salmon.

Bart watched the men setting up the prizes. The bicycle,
of course, held the place of honor on the stand, with the
lesser prizes grouped around it. The red and silver bike
looked even more alluring than ever to Bart, but the certainty of winning it, which he had hugged to his heart for
so many weeks, was fast slipping away from him.

"Seven o'clock," announced Mr. Jensen on the loud-
speaker. "You have three more hours to fish. Be sure to
bring your fish in immediately to be weighed in."

Bart turned away restlessly. One whole hour gone, and
he had not caught a single fish. He moved over to the

counters where the fish would be laid in order of weight. There were only two so far, besides Vic's, both of them small. If only he could hook a big one—and land it, he added, remembering his fouled line.

The crowd of onlookers had increased during the last hour. Hundreds of men and women, young, old and middle-aged, stood on the promenade, gazing out on the harbor. Some had cameras and were taking pictures. A few had binoculars. One man held a home movie camera.

Bart looked out on the bay. From here, the scene was different, and even more impressive than when you were out in the midst of the boats. From the shore the harbor, emerald green in the early morning light, was studded with tiny boats; at this distance their slow movement seemed no motion at all. So many fishermen, and so few fish being caught—and at least two of the fish caught unfairly.

Mrs. Skinner hurried past, a huge coffee pot in her arms.

"Hello, dear. Having any luck?"

Bart shook his head dolefully. "Vic got a small one."

"Have you seen your father and Eddie?"

Again Bart shook his head. He had not seen them since the starting gun. Eddie's name was not on either of the fish on the counter, so he, too, must be having poor luck.

"Don't get too cold, Son," his mother admonished. "You look a bit blue around the lips. Too bad we haven't any cocoa hot yet."

Bart assured her he did not feel cold. But he did. He was not only cold physically; a chilling fear that he would

168

not catch any fish bothered him far more than his icy feet.

"Well, I must get the coffee on," his mother said, resuming her quick progress. "The men who come in from fishing will be wanting some."

As she went on down the promenade to the big outdoor stove, Vic came up, having seen his fish duly weighed and tagged.

"Okay. Let's go."

Bart started for the shore, but turned back on an impulse with a muttered, "Back in a minute." He ran to the microphone where Mr. Jensen stood.

"Did that fellow get a sheer pin for his boat?" he asked.

Lexy's father looked down at him. "No, Bart, he didn't, so far as I know."

Bart fumbled in his shirt pocket. "Well, he might as well use this until I need it."

Mr. Jensen took the tiny strip of metal and smiled. "That's fine, Bart. If you need it, come in to shore and I'll get it back for you."

Bart nodded and ran down to the boat where Vic waited. He'd have to row in if he broke his sheer pin, but that wouldn't be as bad as having to row all the time, like the other fellow was having to do.

"Where did you go?" Vic asked curiously as they pushed the boat out.

"Oh . . ." For some reason Bart was reluctant to disclose his act of generosity.

Over the microphone Mr. Jensen called, "I have a sheer pin now for a 3-horse Johnson. If the man who wanted one will come in to the promenade, he can have it. Repeat: a sheer pin for a 3-horse Johnson now available."

Vic smiled. He nodded approvingly at Bart.

Out in the bay again, the two boys resumed their trolling.

Another hour passed. Frequently they saw other contestants catch fish, one or two of them nice big salmon. But neither Bart nor Vic got even a nibble.

"Want to mooch?" asked Bart at last.

Vic considered, then shook his head. "Let's troll a while longer first. How about trying spoons for a change?"

They made the switch. Still no luck. They saw Lexy, in the boat with Steve, hook a fair-sized silver and net it without a bit of help from her excited, clumsy companion. They saw Dr. Skinner and Eddie pulling for shore. Eddie held up a fish, clutching it in both hands, his eyes glowing, his face shining. Bart thought he had never seen his brother so happy in all his life.

Still their lines trailed in the water, the tips of the rods jerking gently and rhythmically with the action of the lures.

"Rats!" groaned Bart at last. "What's the matter with me today? Can't even get a nibble!"

"I'm not much better," Vic comforted him. "My little trout will probably be at the end of the line."

"At least you might get *some* kind of prize!"

As the minutes stretched out, Bart saw his dream of winning the top prize slip away from him. It looked like he wouldn't win any prize at all, not even the pair of movie tickets that was the last prize.

The skiff was even with the lighthouse now. Time to turn back. If only they could go beyond the lighthouse where he might stand a better chance of hooking a fish, Bart thought. He sighed deeply, and turned the tiller.

Then it happened. His pole bent almost double. A strike!

Afraid to breathe, afraid to yell for fear that somehow his voice would keep the fish from swallowing the hook, Bart tightened his grip on the pole. A quick jerk; it was safely hooked. The line began to spin out with incredible speed.

Vic had drawn in his line immediately. Now he sprang to the tiller and opened up the engine. Both boys recognized instantly, from the force of the strike and the speed of the run, that the fish on the other end of the line was no mere salmon trout.

Bart braced himself for the struggle ahead, clutching the rod for dear life. Fortunately, the fish had headed for deep water, away from interfering boats. Although the motor was wide open, running at full speed, the salmon continued to take line. Bart gulped. If it kept going like this, his line would break, for sure!

Suddenly the line went dead. Bart began to reel in very cautiously. No feel on the line whatever. Maybe the fish had got away! Bart's heart dropped into his boots. Mechanically he continued to crank the reel, but the fear that he had muffed his big chance became a certainty. What had he done wrong? No one had fouled his line this time. No chance that it had caught in the propeller; Vic had handled the boat perfectly. Maybe the hooks had not

171

caught securely; perhaps the salmon had merely been hooked in the edge of the mouth, and he had torn loose.

"What's wrong?" asked Vic anxiously.

"I don't know." Bart's voice shook with disappointment. "I don't like it. There's no pull at all."

The words were scarcely out of his mouth when his rod was almost snatched out of his hands by the force of the salmon's new drive. Again they were off, out in the bay. Bart's hands ached from holding the rod, but his heart leaped with joy. This was a big salmon, and a smart one. He had nearly caught Bart off guard. A victory over this baby would be something to crow about.

For endless minutes the fight went on. Bart was not to be caught napping again. No matter how cleverly the fish played possum, the boy did not relax his grip on the rod.

At last the salmon began to tire; his runs became shorter and shorter. But Bart was tiring, too. What if his strength gave out just as victory was within his grasp? Cautiously he shifted the pole, and held it with his knees as well as with both hands.

"He's almost done for," Vic declared, cutting the motor's speed as Bart reeled in for the sixth time. "You'll land him now, sure."

Bart did not dare to hope. He ached all over. This struggle seemed to have been going on for hours. Over the loudspeaker a voice echoed faintly. Bart could not make out the words at this distance.

"One more hour," Vic interpreted, looking back at the shore. "There's the nine o'clock signal flare."

One more hour! Bart's right hand turned the crank

while his left kept a tight grip on the rod. It seemed to him he had been playing this fish for hours. Could he land it in just another hour?

"There he is!" Vic pointed over the side of the boat.

Yes, there he was, close to the boat, the biggest fish Bart had ever caught. . . . But he hadn't caught this one yet, Bart reminded himself; many a fish got away when he was being netted.

The gaff! Dr. Skinner had given it to Bart instead of taking it himself. Quietly Bart asked Vic to get it.

Steady. Reel in slowly, quietly. Don't scare him now.

Stealthily Vic crept to the bow and got the gaff. On the way back he took up the net, too.

"Want me to gaff him for you?"

Bart considered. Contestants were permitted to have help in gaffing or netting. If he tried to do it alone, tired as he was, he might lose his fish. But somehow, win or lose, he wanted to do this all by himself.

"I think I'd rather do it myself."

Vic nodded. He understood how a fellow felt.

Steeling himself for a surprise move by his quarry, Bart took the gaff from Vic. Steady. Don't be in a hurry. Now! The sharp point found its mark, deep in the gills.

"Nice going!" cried Vic. "You got him!"

And then the fish was in the boat, threshing wildly on the floorboards. A single blow and he lay still.

The two boys pounded each other on the back jubilantly.

"We did it!" screamed Bart.

"What do you mean, 'we'?" howled Vic. "You did it yourself."

"If I hadn't had you to handle the boat . . ." Bart did not need to finish. Both boys knew what a time he would have had alone.

"Let's get this baby in to the scales!" Vic exclaimed, dropping down beside the motor and winding the starting cord around it.

All the way in to shore Vic kept chortling and exclaiming over his companion's catch. Bart said hardly a word. He sat, drained of all feeling, now that the reaction had set in, looking down at the beautiful silver salmon. His hands and arms, relieved of the long strain, felt empty and dead, apart from his body.

What a grand guy Vic was, to be so happy over someone else's good fortune! He could hardly have been happier if he had caught that fish himself. Bart wondered if he could have been so generous, if it had been the other way around.

When they had nearly reached the shore, Bart came to life. Getting a firm grip through the gills of his salmon, he lifted it up. He climbed up on the bow of the boat and stood there, holding his catch aloft, as the skiff swept up on the sand.

"Here comes a big one!" shouted someone on the shore.

On the promenade, Eddie screamed in high delight. "Bart's got a big one! Bart's got a winner!"

Bart's got a winner! The cry sped along the line of spectators. A winner! Bart's got a winner! Barton Skinner! Just look at that fish! He'll get the bicycle, just watch and see!

The words were music to Bart's ears. He smiled happily

Yes, there he was, close to the boat, the biggest fish Bart had ever caught. . . . But he hadn't caught this one yet . . .

at everyone in sight and hurried over to the scales, followed by the entire crowd.

His salmon weighed in at twenty-four pounds, seven ounces. Six pounds heavier than the fish that had previously held the lead!

The admiring crowd pushed close to look over Bart's shoulder.

"You've got a good chance, boy," said the man at the scales, clapping a hand on Bart's shoulder. "They'll have to go some to beat that salmon. Looks like that red bike has your name on it!"

Bart had never been so happy.

19. BART PREPARES A SPEECH

SUDDENLY IT DAWNED ON BART THAT HE had no business wasting time here on shore. He had caught *his* big fish, true; but Vic's catch was too small to give him a chance for a good prize. He had to take his friend out again.

Bart tore himself away from the admiring throng around the display tables and ran down toward his boat. At the edge of the promenade he met Vic.

"I was looking for you," his friend said with his slow smile.

"Yeah. I'm ready. Let's go."

"You don't have to go out again, Bart, unless you really want to. Al hasn't caught a very big one yet, either, so we can team up—that is, if you'll let us take your boat."

"Sure!" Bart grinned, relieved. He wanted Vic to have another chance, but he had had enough fishing, himself, for one day. He was tired, after his long struggle with that salmon. And anyway, he'd like awfully well to stay on

177

shore and see if anybody else brought in a winner. He took off his parka and tossed it in the boat.

Vic and Al shoved off. Bart went back up the promenade, Eddie hovering at his elbow. Their mother came hustling up with her short, brisk step. "I hear you caught a big one, Bart."

He took her over to see it. Her exclamations of surprise and admiration were immensely gratifying, and so were the delight and pride in Eddie's eyes.

Then Dr. Skinner came back from helping to transport the boxes of frankfurters and buns down to the stove.

"Mighty fine fish, Son."

Bart beamed.

"He'll get the bicycle, won't he, Dad?" Eddie's high voice pierced the babble of the noisy crowd.

To Bart's surprise, his father hesitated before he answered. Surely there was little doubt that his fish would win! Of all the long line of salmon laid out on the counters now, neatly tagged with their weight and their owners' names, not one even approached his in size. And there couldn't be more than thirty or forty minutes left to fish.

"Well," Dr. Skinner smiled down at his elder son, "I wouldn't count too much on it, Bart. The Derby isn't over, you know, until the finish signal."

Bart turned away, somewhat dashed. Of course his father was right. Even now, someone out in the bay might be hooking a bigger fish. This last half hour might change the picture completely.

But after a moment his spirits began to rise again. Really, there was very little chance that anyone would top his

178

fish. A salmon that size was not hooked in the harbor every day in the week.

Mrs. Skinner went back down to the stove to get the wieners cooking. Dr. Skinner answered the loud-speaker request for men to string the boats which were no longer needed, and tie them up to the float, ready for their return trip to the boathouse. Eddie ran off to tell some of his schoolmates about the big fish his brother had caught.

Bart wandered up and down on the promenade. The place was alive with people now. Everybody in Harbor City had come out for the finish, whether they had children in the Derby, children too young or too old, or no children at all. Youngsters rode along the promenade on bicycles, periling themselves as well as pedestrians. Babies were pushed in perambulators, or held in their fathers' arms.

Every minute another boat pulled up on shore, bringing another fisherman and another catch. Each time the cry went up, "Here comes another!"

But none of the new arrivals gave Bart a moment's worry. The fish were small, or moderately large at best. Some were cod or sole or dogfish or bullheads. There was even a huge starfish. Why would anyone bring in a thing like that? Yet Bart himself remembered a Derby when so few salmon had been caught that any kind of a fish had won a nice prize. This year, however, would be different. There were already thirty or forty salmon; nothing else had a chance.

And here came a youngster with a ratfish! What an ugly brute, with its great wing-like fins, its wicked looking teeth!

"Only fifteen minutes left!" blared the loud-speaker. "Only fifteen minutes. When you come in, beach your boat between the promenade and the boathouse. Pull boats way up on the shore, so the incoming tide won't wash them away."

Bart smiled to himself. Only fifteen minutes!

"Remember," Mr. Jensen's voice went on, over the microphone, "your fish must be *on the scales* when the finish gun goes off, in order to count. Repeat: you have less than fifteen minutes to get your fish in to shore!"

Bart's heart began to beat faster. Surely he was safe now! He started to think about what he should say when he was called up before the microphone to accept his prize. "My father taught me to fish when I was six years old, and I've been fishing ever since. I've caught a lot of fish, but this is the biggest I ever caught—the biggest anyone in our family ever caught. I used spoon and . . ."

A stranger with a professional-looking camera had been walking around for the past half-hour, asking questions of young and old, bystanders and fishermen alike. Now he stopped to talk to Bart.

The man represented *Vacation Magazine*, Bart learned, and was here to take pictures of the Derby and write it up for his magazine.

Bart was glad he had remembered to get a haircut yesterday; he would look neat in the magazine photos. He answered the man's questions fully and clearly, thinking all the time that his reward for catching that big salmon was going to be bigger than he had anticipated.

A boat raced up on the shore. His own boat, with Vic

and Al. Vic had a fair-sized salmon, but the other boy was empty-handed. Bart ran down to meet them and help beach the boat.

"Nice going, Vic," he congratulated his friend. "Didn't take you long, did it?"

Vic stepped out of the boat and held his fish at arm's length. He surveyed it critically. "Better than my other one, anyway," he drawled. He started up to the scales.

Bart turned to Al. "You going out for another try?"

Al shook his head. "No use. Even if I caught one now, I'd hardly have time to bring it in."

Without offering to help carry the boat up out of reach of the encroaching tide, Al strode off toward some of his cronies, calling back over his shoulder, "Steve hooked a big one, out near the Patrol Boats. I bet he doesn't make it in before the gun."

Bart forgot about beaching the boat. He looked out over the harbor. He had forgotten Steve. All morning long he had not thought of Steve—or of Lexy, either. Had they caught any fish besides the one Lexy had brought in during the first half of the Derby? He had not seen Steve's name on any of the fish lined up on the display counters.

"Ten minutes!" came the warning over the microphone. "Only *ten minutes left!*"

Dr. Skinner strode up the beach. Bart noticed the binoculars dangling from his shoulder.

"Dad! May I use those binoculars?"

"Of course." His father handed him the glasses and went on up the beach to gather up the boats the contestants had finished with.

181

Bart hung the binoculars around his neck and focused them on the north boundary of the Derby. There were very few fishermen left on the bay now; most of them had either caught a fish or given up. Bart had little difficulty in locating Steve's boat.

Steve was standing, legs braced wide apart, hands clutching his pole. No doubt about it, he had a big one. Watching his rival, Bart felt again the strain and the anxiety he had known all during his fight to land his own salmon. Lexy was rowing frantically; her bandana had fallen off and her hair streamed around her face.

Now she stopped rowing. Steve stood still, looking down. He reached one hand toward Lexy, and she held out the net.

Cautiously Steve bent over the far side of the boat. Bart held his breath. Would he make it?

Yes! Steve straightened up, dropping his rod. In the net was a huge flopping fish! But he was going to lose it! The fish was going to jump out! No, Steve moved too fast. Now the fish was out of sight in the boat, and Steve and Lexy stood looking down, their faces shining.

Then Steve dropped down on the rower's seat and snatched the oars. He pulled on them so hard that Lexy nearly toppled over. Hurriedly she took a seat facing him. Steve rowed wildly, furiously. He lifted the oars too high to feather. An oar came out of the oarlock. His clumsy hands fumbled trying to put it back. What happened then Bart could not see clearly, but the next instant the oar dangled crazily. The clumsy fellow! He had broken it!

The binoculars dropped from Bart's hands and dangled

182

on their strap. He bent over, gave his boat a quick, hard shove and jumped in. Two bounds and he had reached the motor. He pushed the propeller into the water with one hand and snatched up the starting rope with the other.

"Five minutes!" roared the loud-speaker. "Only five minutes! *Your fish must be on the scales when the gun sounds!*"

The motor caught instantly and the boat shot through the water. Bart turned the tiller and headed straight for the north boundary of the Derby.

On the shore a yell went up. Bart wondered absently what they were shouting about, but he had no time to look back.

20. THE CRAZIEST STUNT

BART HAD COVERED HALF THE DISTANCE to the north boundary before he realized fully what he was doing. Then he pounded his fist against his knee in exasperation against himself.

Of all the nit-wits! Here he had the Derby sewed up—his fish was by far the biggest yet brought in—still he had deliberately set out to help his rival bring in a salmon which might well top his! How stupid could he get?

Worst of all, it wasn't just anybody he was promoting to Fishing Derby winner over himself. It was Steve, the big newcomer to Harbor City whom he had resented ever since he met him—resented him for his tall, husky body, for his effortless popularity, for winning the cheer leader job, for taking Lexy away from him. Steve, his rival and his enemy, whom he had helped out of trouble time after time.

Well, he wasn't going to help him now. Bart turned the tiller. He would go back in. Let Steve lose out. It would serve him right, the clumsy goon! But instantly Bart brought the boat back on course. No, he would not go back. Steve didn't have a fair chance. He could scarcely have gotten in to shore soon enough with two good oars; rowing that distance in five minutes would be almost impossible. And with a broken oar . . .

The image of the red and silver bicycle rose before Bart's eyes, then the tiny shining trophy, which he had already placed mentally on his dresser at home. He remembered the acceptance speech he had planned, the radio interview that was to come, the pictures in the paper, the photos in *Vacation Magazine*. None of those would now be his. They would all belong to Steve. Stephen Huber would be featured as today's top winner, not Barton Skinner.

No! He wouldn't help Steve. Over and over he had helped the goof. He had taught him how to fish in the first place. He had rescued him from the barge. He had saved him from drowning, even though Steve would not have been in danger if it had not been for Bart's clowning.

And how had Steve repaid him for all that? He had taken Bart's girl. He had snagged the cheer leader job. And now he had caught a fish that might snatch the Derby victory from Bart's grasp. No! He would not help him. He would go back to shore.

All at once Bart noticed in amazement that, even though he had been deciding in his own mind to turn back, his hands had not obeyed. The skiff still headed straight for the boat that drifted helplessly on the blue-green water. Bart shrugged and made no attempt to alter his course again.

Oh, well, he had another year to fish in the Derby, but this was Steve's last opportunity, his first and his last. Another year . . .

Bart was nearly there now. He cut the motor's speed, but did not turn it completely off; no time to waste starting it again.

"Bart!" It was Lexy's voice, high and shrill in relief and joy. "Oh, hurry, Bart!"

Steve was already in the bow, the mooring line in his hand; he had that much sense. He tossed it across the narrow strip of water.

Bart caught the rope and speeded up the engine. He could tie the rope while they were moving. He cut the turn as close as he dared and pointed his stiff toward the promenade.

No one said a word on the return trip. All three urged the boat forward with their minds. Bart could feel the intensity of the others' wish.

"Two minutes!" Bart caught his breath at the warning. Could they make it? What if his crazy trip out here didn't help, after all? He tried to tell himself he would be glad if they were too late. But he knew he would not be. This was Steve's first Kids' Fishing Derby and his last. A fellow ought to have one chance. . . .

"One minute!"

A tremendous shout went up on the shore. For the first time, Bart became aware of the throng on the promenade. Everybody, men, women and children, had congregated to watch the race with time. The stove was deserted. So were the prize platform and the display counters. So were the float and the strings of boats. All of Harbor City stood together in a shouting, whistling mob, cheering for the little

"Two minutes!" Bart caught his breath . . . Could they make it? What if his crazy trip out here didn't help, after all?

skiff and its rescue mission.

Only Mr. Jensen stayed at his post at the microphone.

"Hurry, Bart! Only half a minute! *Hurry!*" His voice roared over the loud-speaker, trembling with excitement.

Bart cut the motor and tilted it out of the water. The keel of the boat grated on the sand. Steve leaped out into the water, hugging his big salmon close. Half a dozen men waded out to meet him.

Steve turned to Bart. "Gee . . ."

Bart interrupted him sharply. "*Run!*" And Steve ran.

The next few seconds were a blur to Bart. Lexy was laughing and shouting, pounding him on the back. The men were pulling in the boat, clapping his shoulder until it hurt. His Dad was smiling at him without a word, then bending over to fumble uselessly with something in the bottom of the boat.

Then the gun went off, and the Harbor City Kids' Fishing Derby was over.

The crowd moved as one man to surround the scales and learn the official weight of Steve's fish. Only Lexy and Dr. Skinner stayed behind with Bart.

Lexy pulled his sleeve. "I haven't got a date yet for the Freshman Hop. If you still want me . . ."

Bart stared at her. How was a fellow expected to understand girls? She hadn't wanted to go with him because he was too small—she didn't like to be "conspicuous." Yet now, when he was just as small as ever, when he was the very same "Half-Pint," she had changed her mind!

"Sure," he managed to say. "Sure, Lexy."

188

He watched her climb the steps to the promenade.

Dr. Skinner looked at his son, started to say something, then he, too, joined the crowd around the scales. Bart lingered alone on the beach.

The loud-speaker crackled, then Mr. Jensen spoke again. "Steve Huber's fish got in just under the wire, and it is a beauty. Twenty-four pounds, eight and a half ounces!"

Bart sighed. An ounce and a half bigger than his. So he had lost the grand prize and all the publicity that went with it—by his own actions, too. And he had lost to the boy he had vowed to beat!

Yet, to his surprise, Bart found he was not sorry. He wouldn't get the bicycle or the public acclaim that would have been his as winner, but he had a fine feeling of warmth and pride in his heart. Maybe he hadn't won, but he had played fair. Old Boone-goon was right, after all; there was something better than winning, and that was self-respect.

Bart squared his shoulders and went up to stand on the fringe of the crowd.

The microphone was down on the speaker's stand now. Mr. Jensen still presided as chairman of the Fishing Derby. "Will the crowd please move back? Back on the grass. We've got to make room for all these fishermen whom we are honoring today."

There was a great bustling and shuffling and pushing; at last a big, clear semi-circle began to form in front of the stand.

"Now all you boys and girls who caught a fish today— any kind of fish—come here and line up."

Bart wormed his way through the crowd. As in any

Steve leaped out into the water, hugging his big salmon

close. Half a dozen men waded out to meet him.

gathering, people towered over him. But today, somehow, he did not feel overpowered or lost. Today he felt a real person, regardless of his size.

He found himself standing next to Steve. In spite of the difference in their height, Bart felt for the first time that they were equals. Their glances held mutual respect—yes, and liking!

The crowd still milled around, each person trying to find a good vantage point from which to watch the ceremonies. Boys climbed up to sit on the window sills of the recreation hall. Fathers held small children on their shoulders. The buzz of excited conversation rose to a shrill babble.

Steve muttered in Bart's ear, "I didn't have a chance to thank you."

"Skip it," Bart replied. And this time he meant it. He didn't want thanks for his help. He would have done the same for anyone, without thought of thanks or reward.

And suddenly Bart knew that was the way it had to be: you did what you could. Some people were good at one thing, and some at another. When you saw someone in trouble, you did what you could to help, no matter who they were, no matter whether you liked them or not. Then maybe some day, when *you* needed help—a different kind of help, perhaps—someone would come to your assistance. You couldn't go around thinking about yourself all the time and forgetting other people, because then . . .

Steve was muttering again. "I haven't told anyone else, Bart, but I want you to know. . . ."

Bart came out of his thoughts and listened.

"Getting that fish in was mighty important to me. You

192

see, it makes me feel like I *belong*."

Bart stared up at him. What on earth was Steve talking about?

"I never belonged anywhere before. In the orphan asylum—so many boys—nobody cared. We never had time for games, no fishing or swimming. Then Mr. Huber . . ." The deep voice went on whispering, reaching no ears but Bart's in the confusion attendant on the preparations for the prize-winning ceremonies.

Bart's eyes widened. Lots of things were becoming clear. Steve hesitating before saying "my Dad." Steve calling his mother "Mrs. Huber." Steve saying "my father's brother," instead of "my uncle."

An orphan! Bart tried to think what it would be like to live in an orphanage with hundreds of other boys. No mother. No dad. No kid brother. No home . . .

"Well, anyway . . ." Steve was still talking. "I wanted you to know I'll never forget it. It was mighty big of you, Bart."

The two boys, one tall and brawny, the other little and lithe, exchanged a long look. Both of them smiled slowly.

"There's nothing small about you," Steve finished, "except your size."

Bart turned his eyes on the crowd. He saw his father watching him. At last he understood what his dad had tried to tell him: there are two kinds of bigness. The physical kind you can't help; you either have it or you don't. But the bigness inside of you—you make *that* yourself. And that's the kind that matters most.

"Ladies and gentlemen," said Mr. Jensen. "And *young*

ladies and gentlemen."

The ceremonies were about to begin. The crowd became quiet.

"The thirteenth annual Harbor City Kids' Fishing Derby has come to a close. It is my pleasure to introduce to you a man who needs no introduction: Mr. Stanley Boone, principal of Harbor High School, who will award the prizes today!"

As Mr. Boone stepped to the microphone, Bart found that he could look at his principal without rancor for the first time in many weeks. He could look any man or boy in the face today.

21. CHEERS FOR BART

"I CAN'T THINK OF ANY TASK I'D RATHER have," Mr. Boone began, "than this one of presenting the prizes to these winners of the Harbor City Kids' Fishing Derby. There's only one thing I don't like about it: that we can't give a prize to every single boy and girl who competed today.

"This Kids' Fishing Derby was started, as most of you know, thirteen years ago by a group of Harbor City residents who believed firmly in two things: they believed that the youth of our country are the hope of its future, and they believed that fishing is a universal and a beneficial sport, one that can be carried on through youth, middle life and old age. This Fishing Derby was inaugurated in order to put into the hands of our young people fishing rods with which to enjoy a good, clean, healthful sport, and to put into their minds and hearts a love of the outdoors and habits of sportsmanship which would go with them throughout their lives."

Bart blinked. He had never stopped to wonder *why* the Fishing Derby had been instituted in Harbor City. He had always just taken it for granted.

"You young people," Mr. Boone went on, "all of you who competed today, and you who are too young, and you who have passed your fifteenth birthday and are no longer eligible—all of you are the sportsmen of tomorrow. We want you to be *good* sportsmen, capable and intelligent. We want you to be interested in the conservation and propagation of fish and wildlife. We want you to grow up to be conscious of the great beauty and resources of the Northwest, and to guard them for the next generation, and the next.

"But more than that, perhaps, we want you to grow up to be *good sports* as well as sportsmen, to learn to be good winners and good losers. In a way, nearly everything in life is like a fishing derby: only one person can get the best job in an office. Only one person can win the election. Sometimes you have good luck, sometimes bad. We can't all be winners, but there's one thing we can be: we can all be good sports.

"Long after the prizes you have won today are worn out or broken, the memory of the Derby will live on in your hearts, the memory of how you fished and the way you won—or lost."

Mr. Boone paused. He looked at the card Mr. Jensen handed to him. The two men whispered together a moment.

"And now," the principal resumed, "I think we have made these young people wait long enough to get their prizes. Will Stephen Huber come up to the microphone, please?"

In spite of himself, Bart winced. If he had not been so all-fired helpful and generous, it would have been *his* name Mr. Boone was calling first. Then he saw Steve's worried frown and he forgot himself. The big fellow was scared!

"Go on," Bart whispered. "You have to go up and get your bike!"

Obediently Steve turned. He stumbled up the steps to the platform. The press photographers got into position for pictures.

"The biggest fish today," announced Mr. Boone, "was caught by Stephen Huber, a newcomer to Harbor City. This is his first fishing derby, I understand. Is that right, Steve?"

"Yes, sir." Steve's voice sounded husky and nervous over the microphone.

"Have you done a lot of fishing?"

"No, sir." Steve's shaky voice almost faded out.

"Did you have any trouble landing this salmon?"

Steve gulped. He gave up trying to speak and merely nodded.

"Did it take you very long?"

Again the boy nodded.

Bart grinned sympathetically. How the poor guy shook! He was scared to death, in front of all these people.

"Is there anything you want to say to your friends and neighbors of Harbor City?"

Steve gulped. "Uh . . . Bart . . . uh . . ." There was a

197

bright flash, and then another, as the photographers took their pictures. The crowd broke into cheers. Steve flushed and hung his head. Amid applause and laughter, Mr. Jensen rolled the bicycle toward him and Steve took it with a muttered "thanks" and got down from the platform, covered with confusion.

Again, at the sight of the beautiful bicycle in Steve's possession, Bart suffered a pang of regret. But the happy light in Steve's eyes, now that he was down from the platform and no longer self-conscious, made it impossible to begrudge him the prize.

Steve rolled the bicycle directly to Bart.

"Barton Skinner!"

The words startled Bart. He looked up. Mr. Boone was calling for him to come to the platform. Why, of course! He would get second prize. He sprang lightly up the steps.

"The second prize," announced Mr. Boone, "goes to Barton Skinner, for a salmon which lacked only one and a half ounces of matching the top prize winner. Have you been fishing long, Bart?"

"Ever since I was six." His voice was clear and confident.

"What kind of lure did you use?"

"Spoon, with eight ounces of lead."

"Were you trolling or mooching?"

"Trolling, with an outboard motor." His answers were quick and concise.

"Where did you catch it?"

"Within a stone's throw of the lighthouse. Just inside the boundary." He smiled, remembering the fish that was caught *outside* the boundary.

"Your prize, Bart, for the second largest fish is this camera with flash attachment. Congratulations!"

Bart thanked him and took the camera. He went down the steps and started to make his way around the crowd.

Mr. Boone's voice stopped him. "Don't go away, anyone. We have a special prize to give when all the regular ones have been presented. Will Alexandra Jensen come up, please?"

The name sounded vaguely familiar to Bart. Alexandra . . . Why, that was Lexy! She must be third prize winner.

Sure enough, Lexy had won the portable radio. She held it up to show him as she came down from the platform and beamed happily.

The rest of the prize-presentation went faster. Mr. Boone did not stop to ask many questions about lure or gear. Fourth prize . . . fifth . . . sixth. Then the "Lucky Seven."

"Edward Skinner."

Bart whistled involuntarily. So Eddie would get his wish! Hurray!

Bart moved closer to the platform to see what the "Lucky Seven" package contained. A beautiful catcher's mitt and a baseball and bat! Eddie's eyes gleamed. He could scarcely find enough voice to express his heartfelt thanks. Bart smiled proudly as his younger brother brought his treasures down from the platform.

Eighth prize . . . ninth . . . tenth . . . eleventh . . . At last all the prizes had been awarded.

Mr. Boone cleared his throat. "Ladies and gentlemen, we have a special award today." He held up the tiny trophy Bart had first seen at the rally. "Originally the committee

199

planned to present this small loving cup to the boy or girl who caught the largest fish, since the trophy was ear-marked for the 'Best Fisherman.'

"However, after thinking it over, the committee concluded that the term 'Best Fisherman' covers more ground than actually hooking and landing a big fish. It includes sportsmanship as well. Now, all of our contestants have been good sports today—well, nearly all . . ."

Bart remembered the boys who had fished beyond the lighthouse, and the girl, Darleen, whose father had landed her fish for her. What had become of her? Now that he thought of it, Bart had neither seen her nor heard her name mentioned in connection with the prizes. Someone must have reported her father, or else he realized his mistake and had not entered the fish.

Mr. Boone went on talking. "But today we have had an outstanding exhibition of sportsmanship, one which I have never seen exceeded. A boy whose fish stood an excellent chance of winning the top prize deliberately threw away that chance to help a rival contestant."

Bart caught his breath. Why, Mr. Boone was talking about *him!* His face grew red.

"So the committee has decided to present this 'Best Fisherman' trophy to the boy whose love of fair play outweighed his desire to win the prize. Barton Skinner!'"

The crowd went wild. They clapped and cheered and whistled. Bart's vision seemed strangely blurred. He stumbled as badly as Steve going up the steps this time. He took the little silver cup from Mr. Boone with an unsteady hand. But he could not get out a single word of thanks; his tongue stuck in his mouth.

Flash bulbs exploded and cameras clicked, as the newspaper photographer and the *Vacation Magazine* man took pictures.

Mr. Boone smiled at the boy and patted his shoulder. "We're proud of you, Bart."

The crowd cheered louder than ever as Bart stumbled down the steps, feeling both proud and humble—and very, very happy.

It was over. The photographers packed up their cameras. The committee began dismantling the platform and the counters. Everybody else adjourned to the big outdoor stove and the picnic tables for hot-dogs and cocoa or coffee.

Someone touched Bart's arm. It was Mr. Boone.

"We've been thinking we could use two yell leaders, Bart, now that our enrollment is getting so large. How would you like to work with Steve on that job?"

Bart looked from Mr. Boone to Steve, who stood right behind him. A month ago Bart would have spurned any suggestion that he work with that big goon. But now . . .

Steve's eager grin decided it.

"I'd like it, Mr. Boone. I think Steve and I can work together okay."

"You bet!" Steve declared. "We'll make a good team."

Bart glanced down at the little trophy in his hands. Yes, they would make a good *team*. He would not be a selfish showoff, seeking the spotlight. He would be a good sport. This little loving cup would stand on his dresser to remind him. He might slip up occasionally, of course; a fellow could not change completely overnight. But now that he knew how good it felt to get genuine respect from people instead of just laughs . . .

His mother came hurrying up. She touched the little trophy gently.

"I'm so proud, Bart." Her eyes were very tender. "This means a lot more than a bicycle."

She smoothed the sleeve of his red zipper jacket. Then she shook him slightly and laughed shakily.

"I declare!" she exclaimed. "I've got to buy you a new jacket right away. You're growing right out of that one!"

Bart looked down at his wrists, afraid to hope. It had been several weeks, he realized with a sense of shock, since he had remembered to look in the mirror for signs of growth.

Why, his mother was right! His wrists extended two inches out of the jacket's sleeves. He had started to grow at last!

ELIZABETH RIDER MONTGOMERY

was born in Huaraz, Peru, the daughter of an American missionary. She attended Western Washington Teachers College and the University of California at Los Angeles.

Mrs. Montgomery began writing while teaching first grade. Being dissatisfied with the primers used, she decided to "write a better one" and she did just that! However, it was seven years before any of her work was published. An established author of books for young readers now, she has numerous books to her credit, including textbooks, as well as plays and articles.

Although writing is Mrs. Montgomery's chief interest, she also enjoys water-color painting, stamp collecting and rug-making. She has made all of the braided rugs in her eight-room house. She likes music, too, but claims to be strictly a novice here.

Mrs. Montgomery now resides in Seattle, Washington, with her husband and young son and daughter.